Sarah's Story

Surviving the Tsunami

J.D. CARSWELL

◆ FriesenPress

One Printers Way
Altona, MB R0G 0B0
Canada

www.friesenpress.com

ISBN
978-1-03-833985-0 (Hardcover)
978-1-03-833984-3 (Paperback)
978-1-03-833986-7 (eBook)

1. FICTION, ACTION & ADVENTURE

Distributed to the trade by The Ingram Book Company

For Judy, Alana, Kyla, Ben and Cam.

-1-

Sarah MacKenzie had been waking up to the sounds of the camp stove being lit and water starting to boil for several weeks now. Usually it was Sam who was up with the first light getting things ready for his father, Pete, who was ill with pancreatic cancer but fighting to the end by attempting to kayak around Vancouver Island. Sarah had met the two Buchanan men many weeks ago near Robson Bight on the other side of the Island. They were trying to do one last adventure together.

After a few seconds of being awake, Sarah remembered that today they were breaking camp really early to paddle out several kilometers into the Pacific to the Humpback Whale feeding grounds they had heard about the day before. The sea state and weather were supposed to be perfect, but she was really nervous about going so far out from land. And then there it was, Sam had the radio on channel 16 to listen to the weather forecasts for today. She'd best get up and listen along with Sam to make sure nothing was missed. Four ears are better than two.

Her sky-blue eyes opened quickly when she heard Pete's voice and she realized she'd be the last one up, a position usually occupied by him. She also observed that it was still dark outside of her tent. When she had dressed and pulled the plug on her downmat she backed out of her tent to find the kitchen area empty, save for the stove heating the water for tea and porridge. Pete and Sam were in their respective tents packing up. This was the multi-tasking ritual procedure practically every morning. Packing and eating brekkie while taking tents down and preparing to pack all the gear into the kayaks.

Sam emerged from his tent with his arms full of dry bags and stuff sacks, "Morning, Sarah. The tide is just starting to fall, got a sec to help get the boats down and we can pack straight away?"

"You bet. So the forecast is still good then?" She hadn't brushed her hair yet and long sandy brown strands with blonde streaks fell randomly over her shoulders and back.

"Exactly as it was when we went to bed. I think we'll be in for a treat today. One of those days you never forget. Special memories called blue moments."

Light was appearing over the mountains of the Big Island to the east of Flores Island. Their camp seemed to get brighter every time they looked up from their tasks. By the time they were ready to launch the sun was getting ready to peak over the top of Catface Mountain.

They set off at a good pace, Pete was quiet but paddled like there was nothing physically wrong with him. After an hour and a half of steady paddling they stopped for a water break. There was still no sign of whales or of the conditions changing. Sarah still felt nervous about being so far from land in her kayak. They had seen several sport fishing boats heading out, which eased her fears a bit. At least they were not alone out here. And eventually the whale watching boats would come out from Tofino. More company would bring more comfort for her. Sam's theory was that the best things in life make you work for them. Then you appreciate them more. She hoped he was correct about that with these humpback whales.

Continuing on for about half an hour Sarah noticed what looked like hundreds of birds, so she got her binoculars out and put them around her neck while Sam and Pete pulled up beside her.

"They're there! Those birds are shearwaters, and I see the water being churned up amongst them." She couldn't contain her excitement and set off at racing speed. The two older men weren't far behind. Soon they were amongst the birds, and two humpbacks were feeding about one hundred meters in front of them, so they rafted up and watched the action. Food and water were passed back and forth between the kayaks.

Pete exclaimed, "This is the best nature TV show I've ever seen! I can imagine Attenborough's voice too!"

Sam replied that, "All we need is popcorn. Sitting here, soaking up the warmth of the sun, eating nuts and apples. Doesn't get better than this!"

"This is heaven!" said Sarah. "I wonder what the poor people are doing today?"

"Not watching humpbacks feed! Look at that!". The old man was enjoying himself as he pointed out a whale lunging skyward with herring flopping out of its mouth with dozens of birds in and around its massive gape.

"It's not even nine o'clock, and look at what we've already seen. There must be over ten of them within eyesight of here!." Sarah felt the warmth grow inside of her from the awe of being in the presence of the greatness of these magnificent animals. She had been feeling sad that their long kayak trip was ending soon, when they reached Tofino. Sarah didn't feel her journey of self-discovery was complete yet. Perhaps it never would be.

Sam brought them back to reality saying, "We've also got to keep an eye on the conditions. I'm worried about being so far from land. As soon as the whale-watching boats start coming, we should go back just in case the afternoon winds come up. You guys!" he shouted, pointing to a ring of bubbles only two kayak lengths away. "Holy shit, get your paddles in the water for..."

Sam never finished his statement as two humpbacks lunged upwards right beside them. Their rorquals were fully extended, and they seemed to swallow half the sea. White foamy water and small fish flipped everywhere, and shearwaters and gulls were all but flying into the mouth of the whales. The two humpbacks just settled back down into the water as they pushed the water through their baleen and back out of their mouths.

"Maybe that will squeeze a dump out of you, Dad!"

"Right here in my kayak! That was too close for comfort. Luckily they are also feeding by drifting with their mouths open into the schools of feed. But it was pretty amazing to see a small version of bubble netting." Pete was already subconsciously back paddling.

"Encroyable!", but Sarah was looking pale, so they decided to move back a bit when a whale blew about fifty feet across their bows. Then it turned and came right by them. It was so close that they could see the one big eye looking up at them and the turned-up mouth that seemingly smiled as the barnacle covered monster slowly slid past them. Sarah couldn't help thinking that perhaps she was being inspected with as much curiosity as she had for the whales. She realized she hadn't taken a breath for quite a while as she gulped in a large mouthful of moist foul smelling, but oxygen-rich, air.

When the whale was gone she said, "That was too much! I didn't even breathe that whole time. Let's go back." And she sucked in another big breath.

Sam made his usual comment about being in the presence of greatness and then added, "Here come the whale watching boats. Sarah's right, let's go back."

Before they could turn around to head back, all the birds rose as one and flew frantically further out to sea. Then it seemed like all the whales were gone, and the sea became eerily still.

"What the hell!", shouted the old man. "This isn't the tide is it?" The swirling ocean quickly swept them further out, and they felt like they were sinking. Sarah felt a strange sensation in the pit of her stomach, as though they were on an elevator that was descending.

Sam shouted, "There's been an earthquake! This is the start of a tidal wave. Keep paddling out!" Two whale watching boats zipped by them heading toward Japan and in panic the two old men set off after them.

Sarah had to pull her skirt on and then dug in her paddle to follow them. But her paddle hit something hard, and the blade broke off. Putting all of her weight on the right side of her kayak allowed the churned- up sea to tip her over. Her first reaction was one of, "What the Hell?". Opening her eyes she realized the humpback right in front of her was what she had broken her paddle on. The cold North Pacific water sharpened her mind into action. She doubted she could right the kayak easily with half a paddle so she pulled the 'holy crap strap' releasing her skirt. She popped out of the cockpit and rose to the surface gasping for air beside her upside down kayak. She hung onto the kayak gasping and sputtering while she regained her wits and started yelling for Sam. Unfortunately, she couldn't even see them so Sarah knew they couldn't hear her, especially with all the water noise around her.

She couldn't see Sam and Pete or anyone else for that matter. She never had felt more alone and it hit her hard that she had to get out of this on her own. In the back of her head a voice told her that she had the skills to do this and another voice closer to her eyes told her she had better do it fast before the hypothermia beast got her. Or if this was the start of a tsunami would the wave get her?

First she had to right the kayak and start getting the water out of the cockpit, but it was a struggle to flip it over. Luckily she kept her pump under bungees on her aft deck which she could easily reach with her right hand. Pumping while in the water was very tiring but soon the kayak rose up in the water as the cockpit slowly was emptied. Oh, for a large bucket, but as she thought that she had the feeling of an elevator rising. The water became very churned up and she felt an energy lump race by her, causing her to stop pumping and hang on tightly. A tremendous sonic boom followed and Sarah turned to watch the huge surge of water attack the island and coast to her east. She felt shocked with butterflies in the stomach area as she started pumping again.

To battle the cold Sarah pulled herself into the cockpit when it was still half full of water hoping her body heat would heat it and the water up as she continued to pump water out. Now she was able to look around better but there weren't any boats in sight and her eyes kept going back toward Catface and the coast. That prolonged boom had to have been the damage caused by the wave she felt go under her. Sarah wondered how high the shallower water near the shore had forced the wave? Finally, she got most of the water out of the kayak so she could put her spray skirt on and trap some heat in the cockpit. Her spare paddle was on her aft deck and she realized she should have got it before she got in the cockpit. Careful to not tip the kayak over again she managed to wedge herself up and turn back enough to get the two halves of the spare. Settling back down into her seat Sarah felt her back telling her it wasn't happy about the position it had been put into. Ignoring it she put the spare paddle halves together and pulled her skirt back on.

After paddling a few minutes she realized she could try her radio. In the end it wasn't worth stopping for, nothing but static. She realized she was thirsty but her water bottle was gone. Her sunglasses, hat and toque were also missing.

She managed to find an apple and the nuts they had been eating earlier, so at least she could get something in her that might satisfy her thirst. Where the hell were Sam and Pete?

She still saw no other life, human or otherwise. Turning her head back to the west Sarah thought she could hear an engine. If there was a boat she needed to make herself more visible so she used her good and broken paddles and her bright red rain jacket to make a flag she could wave. She couldn't paddle while waving her makeshift signal flag, but perhaps they could see her.

The boat grew louder which was a good sign, but seemed to mostly be heading south and away from her. Sarah rose as high as she could, vigorously waving her 'flag'. Her shoulders quickly grew fatigued due to her body being so cold and the boat now was moving away from her to the south. Suddenly she was aware of another boat coming from the northwest. And this one was much closer to shore and to her. Scanning with her binoculars that still hung around her neck suggested this boat was practically coming directly towards her. While she had the binos out she scanned further afield but saw no sign of Sam and Pete. Where were they? Sarah feared the worst for them.

To make sure this boat saw her she started waving again as the engine noise gradually grew louder. Sarah tried the radio again, calling to this approaching boat and to Sam and Pete. Only static answered her hailing. So it was back to waving her makeshift flag to the boat she was positive had seen her and was coming right at her.

Minutes later the Bamfield Mariner 2 pulled up beside her. Sarah felt the relief flood over her as the two women aboard loaded her and her kayak aboard. When they hugged she couldn't hold the tears back as a spasm of relief flooded over her.

"What are you doing out here?" asked the taller of the two. "By the way, I am Natasha, and my partner at the helm is Emily." Natasha was about her age with long light brown hair, brown eyes and tanned skin. Emily was dark-featured with short cropped hair.

"I'm Sarah. I'm so grateful to you two. I thought I might be a gonner. I was paddling with two older gentlemen and we were observing the Humpbacks when the quake and tsunami happened. We got separated and I got dumped when my paddle broke. You didn't see their double kayak?" Her teeth were now chattering, either from shock or the cold or both.

Natasha directed Sarah into the cabin and in a commanding voice said, "Sarah, get those wet clothes off right now. We'll get you some dry ones and put you in a wind suit with some blankets to warm you up. Take everything off!"

Shaking noticeably now Sarah awkwardly did as she was told and put on the sweatpants and fleece she was given but needed help getting socks on and bundling herself into the wind suit. Natasha then sat her down and covered her in a wool blanket with a thermal blanket on top of that.

"Sorry we have no hot tea for you, but this is at least luke-warm from earlier this morning. Drink it all."

Sarah did as she was told and could tell she already felt better inside and out. Her relief was palpable. "So you never saw another kayak?" she asked again.

Natasha looked back to the northwest and said, "No we didn't. Mind you we weren't looking for anybody either. We were probably like everyone else, just trying to figure out what the hell was happening. And then realizing there was a 'quake and the tsunami. Luckily we saw you waving your flag." She scanned the horizon behind them. "No boats at all and the radio is kaput. The tower at Tofino must have got taken out or something like that. I don't know why the radio won't work."

Emily chimed in with, "I have actually seen a couple of sport fishing boats and a whale watching boat who were south of us. They all went in towards Tof City. We have to get back to Bamfield to the Marine Bi Station there."

Natasha added, "I hope it is far enough up the cliff to have not been hit by the tsunami. But we have no idea. We are marine biologists from UVIC and, like you, we were at the feeding grounds. We were mapping the extent of the shoals the herring gather at."

-2-

Natasha picked up the binoculars again to start looking at the ravaged coast. "Emily you won't believe what I'm seeing. I'll take the wheel, have a look."

After a few seconds Emily exclaimed, "Blunden, Bartlett, and Vargas have all been flattened! There is not much left of them now, just some rocky bits." Remembering that they now had a third person aboard she turned toward Sarah to let her see the devastation only to find her sound asleep.

Moving to stand beside Natasha she whispered, "She's asleep. Should we try to take her into Tofino and perhaps she'll meet her friends? If she survived the tsunami there is a good chance they did as well, being that far from shore."

"Good point. I wonder if we can even get in to Tofino. There is so much crap in the water and what will we find left of it when we get there? They will never know how much damage the quake did because the tsunami wiped the coast clean up to fifty or sixty feet above sea level. And most of these coastal towns are built right on the water." After a short pause Natasha, still speaking in a whisper said, "We should try and drop her off in Tofino if we can."

A long silence overtook the cabin. The only sounds were the constant whirr of the twin Volvos out back and the steady light snoring and deep breathing of Sarah. Emily continued to scan the shore as they got to what should have been the southern tip of Vargas Island. She was searching for the entrance to Templar Channel leading in to Tofino. She noticed there was little left of Wickaninnish Island and then she realized what she wasn't seeing.

"Holy crap, 'Tash! Lennard Island lighthouse is gone! Look there at ten o'clock where it should be!".

Natasha let out a gasp and slowed the Bamfield Mariner down to six knots as they encountered more flotsam and jetsam as they approached McKay and Surprise Reefs. Nearing Lennard they saw that the light and all the buildings were smashed and many were not there anymore. The light was split in half, laying ignobly on its side. Templar Channel was full of broken trees and large pieces of buildings. One house looked complete but it was floating upside down in the water. She slowed right down as they started seeing so many trees in the water that she felt she was forced to turn back out again.

"Em, we couldn't get in there if we wanted to or had to. It'll take a number of tide changes to sort that mess out into a channel again. Should we wake Sarah to show her why we can't get to Tofino very easily?"

Emily turned to look at their sleeping kayaker and shook her head, "No, let her sleep. She obviously needs it. I'll take a picture of Templar to show her we couldn't get to Tof City."

"OK. Em, can you take the wheel again? Your eyes are so much better than mine and I am worried about hitting something."

"Fair enough, but I guess we better not go very fast, eh?"

"And we better stay a long way away from shore." Emily knew that they still had a few hours to go yet. And that was only if there were no more surprises. Her mind couldn't stop trying to imagine what would greet them at Bamfield. She was brought back to the present by the radio crackling a bunch of noise followed by silence. She tried calling the Marine Research center but there was no reply.

Sarah became conscious again gasping and spluttering and searching for where she was. Natasha was sitting by her side in a flash comforting her. "You just had a bad dream, Sarah. You are ok now. We've got you safe and sound."

Sarah had stopped gulping air but still seemed confused. "Where are we?", she asked shakily.

Natasha smiled at her as she put her arms around her and replied, "We are near the mouth of Barkley Sound. That far point is Cape Beale and not far from there is Bamfield, where we are trying to go."

"We've gone past Tofino!" Sarah had panic in her voice and she felt sick inside. What about Sam and Pete? Where were they? They weren't going to be at Bamfield and how would she find them now?

"It's ok, Sarah. We couldn't get in to Templer to get to Tofino. It was completely blocked."

It was Emily now, "We took a picture to show you. Check it out."

"Holy shiite! What about my kayak partners? If we couldn't get to Tofino, how will they? I feel terrible." Sarah glared at the photo again. "Look at that mess. I see why you couldn't get through and where is Lennard lighthouse?"

"Gone I'm afraid. And there are no communications, so I think there must be incredible damage at Tofino. We still have our Navigation system so we are still in contact with the satellite. 'Tasha, I'm going to go up to ten knots because the sea is clear ahead and we have lots of diesel."

Sarah felt she had to explain herself, "Look, I'm sorry for my outburst but the two men I was paddling with will go to Tofino looking for me because that was where we were going next. And perhaps ending our many weeks of paddling together."

Natasha asked, "Where did you three paddle from?"

"We met in Johnstone Strait by the Broughton Archipelago. I was on my own and they were attempting to paddle around Vancouver Island as one last adventure together. You see, Pete, the father, had terminal cancer and the son, Sam, was off work due to a medical problem so they decided this would be their last chance to do something like this."

"Wow, that is an incredible undertaking. Why did you join them?"

"They actually started in the Comox Valley. I met them on the beach at Kaikash Creek above Robson Bight watching orcas while we ate our dinners. We got talking and they invited me to share their fire where we would solve all the world's problems every night. I did some day paddles with them and when they moved on I went with them. It's safer with two boats. I guess I was on my own private journey of self-discovery. I just finished my undergrad at UVIC and am trying to figure out what next."

"So you must have some stories, eh?" Natasha was pretty curious about their new boat mate.

"Mostly it was just coping with the conditions and being in awe of the sea and the creatures we saw like bears, orcas, humpbacks, sea otters, wolves, eagles, deer, osprey...well you know. You might have heard about us as we were the kayakers trying to save people at the freighter shipwreck at Rugged Point."

Emily turned back towards them, "Holy crap! That was you! That was all over the news and the Coast Guard and RCMP officers that they interviewed both mentioned you."

"I didn't know that. Sam was always up early and he saw it happen. He and I went out in the double to get as many as we could to shore while Pete worked like a maniac to get fires going to warm them up. The mayday was quickly answered by the people of Kyuquot. On reflection we did everything we could have but at the time it felt so hopeless. Like we couldn't do enough."

"Hey Em, we've got a hero on board!"

"I wouldn't say that. You would have done the same in that situation. Just like you saved me today. A person just does the best they can. I am getting too warm now. I've got dry clothes in the kayak so thanks for these but I think I need some underpants and a sports bra!"

As Sarah got dressed in her own clothes the Bamfield Mariner continued to make good progress heading southeast toward Beale Point.

-3-

Speeding across the mouth of Barkley Sound the world seemed normal, but eerily still and devoid of life and movement. When they turned into Trevor Channel to get to Bamfield all the tranquility changed to chaos. The water was littered with debris and they had to slow right down to pick their way through trees, stumps, and bits of buildings. As they neared Bamfield they came across the roof of a house wedged in a log jam and the forest debris thickened.

Natasha said aloud what they were all thinking, "What if we can't get through?"

Emily, pragmatic as ever, told her, "'Tash, get on the bow with the pike pole and we'll use the pike and the boat to make a channel. Actually, the outgoing tide is already helping us. Look at that opening ahead at two o'clock."

Soon they could see the Marine station appearing to be safe and sound on the top of the cliff which allowed their spirits to rise a bit. Natasha was able to move many trees aside until they got to the mouth of Bamfield Inlet to find that two other boats were ahead of them clearing a route in. The homes on West Bamfield were all destroyed. Bamfield had been a unique community divided in half by the inlet which meant everyone got around by boat so the docks had been crucial to daily life. There had never been roads to the west side. The peninsula looked like Sarah always imagined Hiroshima must have looked like in 1945 after being nuked. The town side of the bay was demarcated by a definite line most of the way up the hill. Above the line were intact buildings with trees and powerlines. Below the line everything was either gone or destroyed. A terrible scar on the land that went to the end of the bay, through the swampy area and beyond.

Natasha shouted back to Emily, "As we thought, the docks are gone. Where should we tie up and try to get to land?"

They had got close to the boat ahead of them, so Natasha asked them what their plan was. Their skipper pointed out that he thought they could tie together, drop anchors and run two lines to shore with their zodiacs. He thought a good spot might be where the main road had come down to the government dock. Together they worked as close to land as they could get and helped each other turn away from the shore to drop their anchors. Running spring lines to shore was a little harder because of all the debris and the difficulty finding something solid to tie to. A large boulder and a concrete road divider flipped on its side did the trick. Strangely nobody from the town came down to help them. Sarah thought they were probably too busy dealing with the aftermath of the big quake to even notice boats coming in.

Emily, Natasha and Sarah each grabbed a couple of bags and headed for the Marine station not knowing what to expect. To get there they had to wind their way through the rubble over what they thought was the road. What should have been a few minutes' walk took twenty minutes to crest the hill and get away from the tsunami debris. Amazingly some buildings looked intact while others were flattened by the quake. All brick chimneys had crashed down, thereby damaging the roofs. Shocked people were sorting out their houses and possessions. Some just sat amongst the rubble with dumbfounded hopeless looks on their faces. Few words were exchanged except at one house where the firefighters and police were trying to free an elderly woman from the basement of her collapsed house.

At the Marine Station they were met by another police car and a terrible scene. The tsunami hadn't gotten this high but the quake had knocked walls sideways so the roof collapsed on all that was under it. Natasha and Emily quickly found colleagues who were distraught because they were in the wooden cabins when the quake happened, but they had friends they were sure were under the collapsed roof. The police asked for quiet and they heard a voice on the far side of the pile. Everybody ran to the other side and started moving building parts aside. Natasha knew the trapped girl and was talking to her.

Natasha explained to the RCMP officer that the trapped girl, Bridget, was fine except for her right leg which was trapped under the edge of one of their specimen tanks. He explained to them all to be careful removing things so they didn't spill more on Bridget. He told them an excavator was on its way and the firefighters and an engineer would be there after they finished the house they were presently working on.

"Bridge, is anyone else under there with you?", asked Natasha.

"Dr. Cummings was in her office and Taylor was working on the abalone tanks." The reply was still strong but they could sense the emotion in Bridget's voice.

Officer Lloyd turned to Natasha and said, "Where would the office be?"

She replied, pointing to the other side of the wreckage, "Dr. Cummings' office was over there at the back of the station, and the abalone tanks were right beside it if Taylor was there."

"OK Good. We'll direct our searches in those areas and try not to disturb what is left of the structure. You three can continue to try to free Bridget. But be careful. One piece at a time. and if anything shifts you stop and tell me. See if you can get her some water and food." Officer Lloyd was a tall clean-cut, take-charge guy, used to giving orders. Everything about him bespoke a person in control. In command. It was almost as if he dealt with huge disasters like this all the time.

They were able to remove some siding and plywood that allowed them to see Bridget because there were eight of them working together now.

Natasha exclaimed, "Bridge, we can see you! We're going to get you out of there! Do you need water or food? We can try to get it in there to you."

"Tash, incredibly I had a flask of coffee in my hand when the quake hit. So I'm still fine and what are you whale people doing here?"

"We were out to sea and so the quake and tsunami barely affected us. Are you warm enough?"

There was a pause and a then a sobbing Bridget replied, "I think I've been through all the stages of shock. I thought I was not going to make it. I wondered if anyone would be around to find us. I passed out for, I don't know how long. When I came to, I hoped the people in the cabins would be safe in their beds and come and find us. But what took them so long?"

Natasha looked at some of them and reported back, "They were in town at the cafe having brekkie and only got here just before we did. Lloyd had told us to be careful not to spill more on you so that is why we're coming at you from the outside wall. An excavator is here now."

"How will it help to get me out?"

"Bridget, there is a beam just above you and I don't think you will be able to move until that tank is moved off your leg. Can you feel your leg?"

"Not really. I guess I'm lucky not to be feeling more pain."

"Bridget, they are going to raise the beam now, if you are ready. They want you to cover your head with your arms."

And so the extraction began with the bucket of the excavator being used like a crane to gently raise the beam after it was secured with a chain. Next the tank was raised about a foot off of Bridget. She had trouble moving away and a fireman had to work his way down to her where he discovered that her leg was crushed with many suspected broken bones in her foot and ankle area. Fortunately, she had no compound fractures. The only blood she had lost was from small surface cuts and scrapes. The fireman used some broken wood and duct tape to immobilize her lower leg as best he could, but Sarah still felt it flopped around like a jellyfish as he slowly moved Bridget. Sarah's stomach was queasy and not for the first time today. As Bridget was slowly passed from hand to hand Sarah noticed that she had lost consciousness. The rescue teams had the substantial task of getting the seriously injured, like Bridget, all the way to Port Alberni if the roads were passable, which nobody knew as yet.

Natasha grabbed Sarah by the elbow, "You alright?" Receiving a nod she continued, "Just heard that Taylor and Dr. Cummings have been found. They didn't make it." Natasha had tears running down her cheeks.

"Oh my god!" Now Sarah felt like she would vomit but was too busy trying to catch her breathe to do so. She sat, head in hands, on a log on the edge of the woods. Natasha joined her in stereo stunned silence.

A cabin was found for Sarah and the surreal day ended with her going for a long sleep on an empty stomach. Her adrenalin had run out and she had nothing left to give.

-4-

First light slowly and gently woke her up. It took her longer than usual to realize where she was but reality did start returning. The experience of the past two days was far from anything she had ever known. It was like being in a dream, or a movie, only it was real. Sarah had no idea what today would bring for her but she did know that she was very hungry, needed some tea or coffee and a visit to the toilet. Her days of going to the right side of the beach were over.

Just as her right foot emerged from her cocoon of blankets, the door of the cabin hesitantly opened. It was Natasha, and like a mind reader, she had two cups of steaming hot coffee with her. Sarah told her to come in and thanked her for the coffee.

After sitting down Natasha said, "Wow, you slept more than fifteen hours! Or were you asleep that whole time?"

"I think I was asleep right through until about ten minutes ago. My body and mind must have really needed it." After a pause Sarah added, "You know what, I don't even remember having any dreams or thoughts of all the horrible things that happened or that I saw yesterday. I sure had them when I dozed after you rescued me."

"Sarah, the Tully came into the channel late last night."

"What is the Tully?"

"It is the John P. Tully, a Canadian Coast Guard scientific research vessel that is leaving to go back to Victoria at 10:00 today. They said they would take any injured and other displaced people back with them. I informed them about you, and the skipper said they could easily take you and your kayak. Interested?"

"Hmm, I um… you know, of course I need to find out what has happened to my parents and their house in James Bay."

"But you hesitate."

"Because I need to find out whether my paddling partners, Sam and Pete, have been found."

"Sarah, we can use the RCMP radio to contact the Tofino RCMP and find out if they know anything. They will have satellite phone contact."

"Great, let's go and then I'll talk to the Tully."

Sarah quickly went to use the facilities and splash some water on her face, got dressed and they were down the road to the small RCMP station. As it was early morning the station seemed abandoned. At least it was undamaged and the door was open. A yawning young, half-dressed cop walked in surprised to see them. After explaining what they wanted he appeared glad to have a mission he knew he could complete. Sarah and Natasha could hear the whole conversation and when Tofino found the names of Sam and Pete on their survivors list Sarah fell to her knees and burst into tears. Sarah missed the rest of the call, so later Natasha explained that Sam and Pete had gone to Port Alberni to get back to the Comox Valley.

The knowledge Sam and Pete were safe allowed Sarah to decide to go to the Coast Guard ship and see if they still had room for her. She realized her mind would never be at ease until she found out what had happened with her parents. So that was her next step. She couldn't do much here and could see that in time she might even be a food and lodging burden in a place she didn't belong.

A mate on the Tully told her they had room, but she needed to hurry because they were already mostly loaded and the captain wanted to leave earlier than planned as they were needed down island. Natasha helped Sarah get her kayak to a zodiac that would run her out to the Tully. An emotional goodbye with Natasha followed for Sarah really felt she and Emily had saved her life. How can one thank someone enough for that gift of life?

-5-

The Tully pulled anchor an hour and a half before the scheduled departure. The air was still and the sea was flat, almost like mother nature was saying she'd give everyone a break for a bit after what she'd thrown at them recently. Sarah ended up being positioned in the galley, which was a reminder that she had not eaten much for two days. The crew kept feeding her and the half dozen other injured people there until she felt one more pancake or cup of coffee would cause her to burst. She still felt she was in a state of head fog divorced from reality. So this was what the word surreal actually meant!

She learned the more seriously injured people were in the ship's infirmary or the twenty spare berths the Tully had to offer. Later in the day Sarah discovered that Bridget was there, and was in serious but stable condition and couldn't be visited.

The Tully was eighty-three meters in length and moved through the sea like a hot knife through butter. As Sarah walked about the ship she saw how well designed it was for its purpose, which was not as a rescue vessel. Needs must so the crew and scientists were doing the best they could to accommodate their unexpected guests by moving gear and projects to make better use of space.

In what seemed like a couple of hours they arrived at Port Renfrew. Even though the town itself was well sheltered up the inlet of Port San Juan, they were greeted with the same tsunami-damaged scene Sarah had experienced at Bamfield. In this bay they didn't even drop anchor to receive the zodiacs delivering a dozen more severely injured people and two paramedics for the Coast Guard to deliver to hospital in Victoria. From the foredeck Sarah could see the extent of the damage to the dock area and up into what had been the town of Port Renfrew. Many of the wooden buildings of Port Renfrew might have survived the quake but the massive water surges of the tsunami had removed most things in their path and either placed them further inland or taken them back to sea. There were boats deposited at the edge of the standing forest and the remains of houses floated around them in the bay. Sarah thought the whole scene was like a scene from a Fellini film, not like the real world.

An hour later they were on their way again. Sarah decided to stay on the foredeck where she was joined by two young crew members, Matt, and Jen, who was part of the science team and seemed to know a lot about earthquakes. Sarah thought Jen looked familiar so she decided to take the chance and ask her. "Jen, I feel like I have seen you before. Did you go to UVIC?".

"Yeah, I did. And still am. I'm doing a masters in environmental studies. Did you go there?"

"Gradded in the Spring. Loved it there."

"What did you study?"

"English. Nothing important and useful like you."

"It's Sarah, right?" Receiving a nod Jen continued, "Hey, people should still be able to study what they are passionate about."

Matt had been standing between the two women and felt like he was a wall between them as they talked around him. He extricated himself and resumed leaning on the rail on the other side of Jen. Bored with their university conversation he started scanning the shore with his binoculars. South of Sombrio Point he thought he could see a change in the damaged coast. In a conversational lull Matt asked, "Jen, and you too Sarah, look at the damaged coast now. Does it seem different to you?"

Jen had her own binoculars so Matt handed his to Sarah who asked, "What am I looking for?"

"I'm not saying. Just want to see if you two notice what I think I do."

Jen smiled. "He's like that. But Matt, you might have something. I don't think the damage goes as far inland as it did at Tofino or Bamfield."

"Ha! I'm not losing it." Matt had a wide grin on his face and Sarah realized she hadn't seen a smile in a few days. She was also aware Matt was overjoyed to notice something before Jen did.

Sarah wasn't convinced which got Jen explaining why Matt was probably correct. "The tsunami came from the Cascadia subduction zone off the coast and as it moved toward the Island, Cape Flattery and the Olympic Peninsula would block some of the force from striking the Island. Victoria is even more protected, so in theory, the tsunami surge should be about half what Bamfield and Tofino got."

Sarah gave a low sound from her belly, "Hummph. So if Tofino got a ten meter tsunami, Victoria should be five?"

"That's correct. But we'll see when we get there later today."

"My parents live in the family home on Dallas Road in James Bay. It was my grandparents' house and looks right over Ogden Point."

Matt broke the silence that followed, "You must be frightened about what you'll find when we get there."

"I can't get it out of my mind. If the house survived the quake would a lower surge like Jen says hit it? I guess I'll find out soon enough."

-6-

There wasn't a lot more to see over the next couple of hours. Sarah, Jen, and Matt stayed on the foredeck watching the shoreline, and as they neared Sooke, others started to join them. To their southeast they started to see a darker, cloudy or foggy area of the sky that none of them took much notice of. Matt had disappeared for a while returning with scones and coffees making it easier to stay outside and watch. The Tully was about 250 feet long and 48 feet wide providing lots of room for people to stand and observe. Jen and Matt had been correct in the tsunami surge only appearing to be five to six meters at Sooke.

Assessing damage at Sooke was difficult because the harbour is very well sheltered. Some houses on the coast seemed to be ok while others, lower down, appeared totally ruined. The Tully had to go out further from land around Beechey Head and Race Rocks making it harder still to ascertain the height of the tsunami and the amount of damage. The cloud to their left grew thicker and more intense like the forest fire smoke they had all become familiar with the past few summers. Once around Race Rocks Esquimalt and Victoria started to come into view. The source of the smokey cloud was now obvious.

All over the Lower Island they could see too many plumes of smoke to count. Amid the gasps and drawn in breathes Jen explained, "The quake must have broken many gas lines. Just as the models predicted."

"So some of the gas leaks ignited burning down buildings and houses rather like the famous quake in San Francisco in the early 1900's." Sarah was gobsmacked at what they were seeing. When she looked at the other faces around her she saw shock and fear. By now they were all prepared for quake and tsunami damage but were not mentally ready for much of the city to have burned as well. Her mind was frantic with fear for her parents and their home she knew had been converted to a gas furnace years ago.

Matt broke the silence that had overtaken them, probably punctuating what they were all thinking, "Holy shit! I was sure we'd be greeted with a disaster. But not this. What will we find left of Vic?"

The captain's voice came on the speaker above them telling all crew to report to the bridge. He always sounded so calm. Sarah and a few others were left behind to ponder what the rest of their day would entail. She was told that the crew were getting instructions for their landing and departure. Sarah wondered what they would do with her and her kayak because unlike most of the guests she didn't need medical attention. The tsunami damage did appear to be about five meters up from the shore, however her eyes now were mostly drawn to the flumes of smoke rising above that line.

The Tully slowed progressively as they rounded Race Rocks and headed for Esquimalt Harbour. Sarah couldn't help but notice the crew racing about readying things for the end of their trip. Nearing the entrance to CFB Esquimalt the Tully came to a stop. A medivac helicopter came out of the smog and gently touched down on their landing pad. Stretchers quickly materialized from the guts of the ship and some of the worst injured were carefully but quickly loaded for the short flight to Victoria General. Zodiacs and one life raft took the rest of the injured ashore to waiting ambulances and vans. There weren't even enough ambulances to accommodate them all. Sarah felt helpless watching this all unfold. She had been told to stay put, out of the way, but inactivity was not in her nature.

Matt approached her, "You are the last of our guests. Where are you going to go?"

"I could get off with your crew at the Coast Guard base. My family lives on Dallas Road."

"We can't do that. The base apparently ain't no more. And it is up the peninsula by Sidney. Anyways we now have to go to Vancouver to help out there."

"Right." Sarah hadn't thought about the Coast Guard base being ruined. "Can me and my kayak disembark from here?"

"Easy peasy! The skipper kind of hoped you'd say that. We'll lower you in your kayak on a pallet. Come with me."

Sarah trailed behind Matt to where her kayak was already loaded on a pallet looking like a fish out of water. He explained that he'd told the captain that she was from Victoria so they had already got ready to off load her.

Finding out she had no more gear he helped her put her paddle together, close both hatches, and put her skirt on after getting into the kayak. As she was lowered into the water Matt wished her a safe journey before going back to work.

As the pallet sunk into the water Sarah could feel her kayak becoming buoyant. Two strokes of her paddle, and she was clear and free. Turning back she signaled to the hoist operator with a thumbs up and thanked him. Matt and Jen were nowhere in sight. She had less than an hour's paddle ahead of her to get to Ogden Point Breakwater where she thought she'd get out to walk to her parents' house on Dallas Road. She started paddling hard, adrenaline pulling her quickly to discover what was ahead. She felt like a horse heading to the barn.

-7-

Approaching the Ogden Point breakwater got increasingly disturbing as earthquake and tsunami destruction became more apparent. The docks were all gone or destroyed. Large ships laid on their sides on Dallas Road and beyond, and houses and trees were all knocked over. Sarah was now sure her family home would be gone from its position across the road. Paddling around the smashed up breakwater to the eastern side she ran into a thick accumulation of rubble and trees. The restaurant and buildings that were there had been wiped off the earth. The whole row of homes that should have been across Dallas Road were gone as she suspected, but what about her parents'?

The currents at Clover Point had created a break in the debris Sarah hoped would afford her a place to land. As she paddled to the point she noticed many people working around the sites of buildings across the street. Two teenagers had seen her and came down to help her land. The taller pocked-marked one asked, "Where did you come from?"

"I just got off the Coast Guard ship, the Tully."

"Oh. Why you coming here?"

"Do you know the MacKenzie house? That's my parents."

"Oh. You're coming to check on them. I see. Want to take your kayak up there?"

"Sure. Thanks for the help."

"It's nothing, don't expect to find much when we get there."

Sarah put her paddle, life jacket and spray skirt in the cockpit, while the two lads insisted on grabbing the bow and stern handles to carry the kayak up to the paths and then to where the road had been. She knew about where the house had been but it was initially hard to tell. As they walked back toward the breakwater, Sarah recognized the next-door neighbours who were sorting through the remains of their home. She instructed the boys where to place the kayak on what had to be the MacKenzie land and thanked the teens, apologizing that she had nothing to repay them for their kindness. They were gone before she realized she didn't even get their names.

Sarah felt her shoulders sink as the enormity of what she was looking at hit her like the proverbial ton of bricks. Sadness and helplessness weighed heavily on her whole body until she sank to the ground too upset to move or stop the tears. The previous surrealness was replaced with a horrible reality. Arms around her shoulders giving her a huge hug brought her back to the present.

"Sarah, you're here!" It was old Mrs. Murray from next-door. Sarah had known her all her life. "I know it's terrible, dearie. Don't cry. You're ok...." Mrs. Murray continued to comfort Sarah and purr sweet nothings into her ear. Sarah couldn't stop sobbing even though the warmth of the neighbour did ease her mind and make her feel better.

Several minutes later Sarah was out of tears and thanked Mrs. Murray as they helped each other to their feet. "Mrs. Murray, do you know where Mom and Dad are?"

"No dearie. We haven't seen them. Perhaps they have gone to your uncle out on the Peninsula."

"But the car is there." Sarah was pointing to a pile of bricks and timbers with the red fender of a car protruding out into the light.

"You are correct, dearie. I'd not noticed that. The authorities came around this morning trying to find people and assess things. They didn't spend much time or find anything at yours. They did tell us they have set up a survivors center at the arena where we can get food and help. It will take a long time before anyone can rebuild or claim insurance or whatnot. They said the government would have to remuster from summer holidays to start to sort it all out."

"What a nightmare." After some reflection Sarah asked, "Where are you two staying?"

"Right here, Sarah. We have our little Boler out back. We had to flip it right side up and clean it out. But the two of us fit in it to sleep and we've got a stove top. You can join us for dinner tonight. The Baker brothers that helped you with the kayak told us the Thrifty Foods in James Bay didn't get too damaged, and hopes to open soon so we'll be able to get food and water. They just have to clean up all the broken glass, and board up holes to stop looters."

"So we're already seeing the worst of humanity after all we've been through."

."Dearie, that element is always there. We're seeing more of the best of people than the other side. Even though most of us down here have lost everything, people from less damaged areas inland are coming to help. Tomorrow an excavator is coming from Colwood to clear roads around here. I can't imagine he'll get paid."

"Well, I guess it makes sense for me to clear an area to set up my tent and I think I'll do the same as you."

"Fine. Dinner in an hour. Just come around back."

"Thanks so much Mrs. Murray."

Sarah found an area at the back of the property that she could easily clear and set up camp. She emptied the kayak and moved it back there as well for protection from undesirables. Mrs. Murray called out for dinner. Since the fence was down Sarah simply walked over it to the makeshift table Mr. Murray had set up. Dinner was a soupy goulash that Mrs. Murray apologized repeatedly for. For Sarah it was perfect for she had hardly eaten or drank anything since she first got on the Tully. They wouldn't let her help with dishes because Mr. Murray was taking them to the sea to wash. The Bolers' water was being saved for drinking. Sarah excused herself to get ready for bed. She suspected sleep would come easily for she was physically and mentally knackered.

-8-

A loud scraping sound brought Sarah rushing back to consciousness in a panic like she had slept through her alarm. She had set no alarm but with her one open eye her watch told her it was nearly nine-thirty. Her inner voice was chastising her for her lethargy while her body claimed it needed to stay cocooned in her sleeping bag all day. The inner critic thought she was a coward who didn't want to face the waste of the yard or go to try and find her family. After more ground shaking from the excavator on the street her inner critic won out and she decided to start moving.

As soon as she poked her head out of her tent Mrs. Murray had a cup of coffee in her hand. "Mrs. Murray, you are a sweetheart. Good morning."

"It is nothing, dearie. Good morning to you. Sleep well?" Even in the worst possible times Mrs. Murray was wearing a dress with a light flower print and seemed as chipper as ever.

"I did. Slept right through until that machine started up. At first I thought the ground rumbling was aftershocks."

"We've had lots of them, although I haven't felt any today. If you need to use the little ladies' room, Kenneth has dug a latrine out back. It's private, and he even found a toilet seat to use."

"You people are the best. Thanks so much."

Sarah couldn't even figure out where to start on their property so she decided that she should prioritize finding her parents first. She figured it would take around thirty minutes to walk across James Bay and up to the arena on Blanshard. She would take Government Street from Dallas Road and see how it went.

Walking along Government was a good choice because it had been cleared. What slowed her down was stopping to look at damaged buildings. Some wooden houses didn't look that damaged, although fallen chimneys had caused lots of havoc. Some had burned to the ground without effecting their neighbour. One whole block was still a smoking burn pile. Brick buildings were basically rubble piles with the remains of a roof on top like a collapsed cake.

A cacophony of noise met Sarah as she approached the harbour. The Parliament buildings were no longer standing there but many people and machines were at work on the site. A paramedic high on the pile raised his arms and everything went still and quiet. Sarah realized they were still rescuing people. This disaster just got worse and worse. She heard the man say that there were four people under him and they needed people and machines to move the stones carefully one at a time. Across the street the Provincial Museum was now mostly underwater although the building was roughly still intact. An older man looking at it told her the earthquake had caused it to sink several feet before the tsunami arrived twenty minutes later to fill the hole in with salt water. He looked so defeated and sad. Obviously the museum had been important to him, but she dared not ask him about it. In a low voice choked with emotion he said, "The world's largest collection of Emily Carr paintings was in there."

"Holy shit!" Sarah couldn't think of how to comfort him and simply moved away feeling helpless.

As she moved further down the hill, Sarah was halted by sea water. She remembered learning in school that this was all reclaimed land that had once been an ocean-side swamp. Looking across to where the Empress had stood she saw a scene worse than that at the Parliament Buildings. It was as if Mother Nature had decided to reclaim the swamp as her own. Where the hotel had stood was now a salt water lake with an island of stone, wood and metal in the middle. Behind the island was another pile where the Crystal Gardens had been. All the glass was gone, and only the odd rib stuck out of the water like the bones of a beached whale or the exposed skeleton of a dinosaur.

Sarah had no idea how long she had stood there dumbfounded by the new face of downtown Victoria, but her inner voice reminded her of today's mission and the fact she couldn't get there this way. She'd have to go back up Government, then over to Beacon Hill Park to the higher ground that would allow her to get to the freshly cleared Blanshard and up to the arena.

Older buildings like the Royal Theatre, the brick churches, and the Dominion Hotel had collapsed from the quake. The few earthquake-designed and repaired buildings were at least standing with all their glass missing and piled below them. Sarah wondered how many of the standing buildings were even usable anymore. All those warnings of how unprepared we were for a disaster like this kept going around in her head. She was seeing exactly how unprepared we had been.

At the top of the rise the arena stood defiantly as if to say to the universe, "Is that all you've got?" The old Memorial Arena would not have survived but this version had been designed to be earthquake resistant. Luckily it had worked although it also had the broken glass problem. At the main entrance, Sarah was met by a Red Cross worker who directed her to where she could find out about missing people. She also made sure Sarah had a place to stay, and informed her where to go for a hot meal. This seemed so well organized compared to the chaos she had just walked through.

City employees, police, and volunteers rushed in all directions in front of Sarah while she made her way to the missing persons section set up on the floor of the arena. Lists of deceased people lined the hallways with frantic frightened people lined up in front of them. When she made it to within sight of the Mac's she couldn't see her parents' names so she moved on to the line up to get to the help desk. The woman helping Sarah had her public library nametag on. Sarah was struck by how calm and efficient Reshmi was in a time like this. Reshmi was a tall thin woman with long dark hair pulled back in a pony tail. In the end Reshmi could only tell Sarah that her area had been searched, that her parents had not reported in as people had been requested to do, and she added them to the list of the missing.

In a mental fog, not for the first time since the earthquake, Sarah started to walk back the way she had come when she remembered about her Uncle Dan and Aunt Sylvia. Not her favorite people, but she went back to find out about them regardless. She turned to cold stone when she found their names on the deceased list. Dan Lewis followed by Sylvia Lewis in black and white staring off the sheets at her. Her Mom's brother and sister-in-law.

"You alright?" It was the Red Cross worker she'd met earlier. Sarah couldn't answer and she didn't know why. She didn't really know or like Dan and Sylvia. "Come with me, we've got a quiet room with refreshments for you. My name is Trini."

With a will of their own Sarah felt her legs follow Trini and sit down beside her when she was instructed to. Trini got her the coffee she asked for and a Nanaimo bar. "Can I ask who you found on the lists? You've not told me your name."

"Sorry. It's Sarah. I was looking for my parents, but they are still missing. I had just found my aunt and uncle."

"I am so sorry, Sarah. Hopefully we'll find your family in the days ahead. It is still so chaotic and crazy here."

"Not just here. Everywhere. One minute it is a beautiful sunny day. The next minute the world is turned upside down. Our lives changed forever."

"Actually, it shook for over three minutes in Victoria. And twenty minutes later the tsunami hit the coast to finish the job. They are saying this is the biggest quake ever recorded. Bigger than the one on January twenty-sixth, 1700. They call it a megathrust subduction quake. Apparently, Victoria has sunk over a meter. The tsunami hit Japan, Korea, and the Philippines all the way across the Pacific."

"Trini, how do you do this all day? Don't you get bummed out?"

"Sometimes. But you also see the good side of humanity. If I help one person a day it is worth it."

"Well, you've made me feel better just talking about this. Or maybe it's the Nanaimo Bar and coffee combo!" Sarah joked for the first time in days. "Thanks, Trini."

After Trini left, Sarah stayed put for a quarter of an hour just thinking and reflecting. Her mind took her back to kayaking with whales and all hell breaking loose. At least she knew Pete and Sam were ok, but would she ever even see them again? It would take many months to fix the Inland Island Highway. There wasn't even phone service yet. Ninety-five percent of the sewage pipes in Victoria were broken so there were not even toilets or running water in most places. It was going to take years to get back to "normal". Sarah knew she had to get over herself and be more like Trini in this new reality or she'd just sink to the bottom like a rock thrown into the ocean. With that thought she got up, returned her cup and headed back to the comfort of her tent.

-9-

Was that Sam calling out, "Daylight in the swamp."? No, just a dream. Sarah opened her eyes to faint light and the start of a new day. She had serious need of a pee and was famished, realizing she hadn't eaten last night. She'd just gone to bed after the sensory overload of the day.

Sarah realized she had been dreaming in that semiconscious state between sleep and awake. She still remembered the vision of an angry Mother Nature explaining to her why all the devastation Sarah had seen the day before had had to happen. The ghostly apparition had said she had to teach humanity a lesson about upsetting the sacred balance of nature. She claimed that humans had ignored her previous warnings of forest fires, droughts, floods, and hurricanes, such that Mother felt she needed to send an even stronger message before it was too late for life on earth. Consequently, she had decided that the biggest earthquake and tsunami the humans had ever seen would get the correct response. Sarah, fully awake and dressed now, wasn't so sure, but the dream was over, and she couldn't dialogue with Mother Nature any more.

After a visit to the loo next-door she started her stove and put on a pot of water. She still stored her food in the safety of the kayak forward hatch. Once opened, the bare spaces indicated it was almost empty. Porridge and tea bags for another week, two cans of tuna, one onion, pasta and rice for a few meals, and one jar of pesto was about all that was left. That would do for today but now she needed to go grocery shopping . Her other mission today would be to start going through the house wreckage to ascertain what she could salvage. Operation salvage would begin today. Perhaps she could find her old bike which should have been in the basement. It would be very useful for getting around right at the moment.

Walking west on Dallas Road Sarah started to become aware that many houses had been moved as a structure to the back and east of their foundations. She asked a workman about it and found out that many of the older homes in Victoria were not bolted to their foundations. It was amazing the inadequacies this earthquake and tsunami exposed about our practices. Sarah was bewildered by the size of some of the ships and float houses that were now located far inland. Fisherman's Wharf had a new address. Heck, it might have a new postal code! She smiled at the thought. Her inner voice still had a sense of humour, even if it thought Mother Nature, from her dream, was probably correct.

Looking up and into the harbour the Johnson Street bridge caught her eye, because something was not right. She realized the bright blue upgraded bridge was still standing out in the days' brilliant sunshine but the on/off ramps were missing from each end. The tsunami must have taken them away. The old buildings on Wharf Street all had collapsed and been washed over. With the new shoreline she would have to walk the long way around to look closer at the damage to Bastion Square, Market Square, and Chinatown, so she decided to just observe from where she was above the site of the former Laurel Point Inn.

Moving back into James Bay she went to Thrifty Foods. It was open, but it had no power or internet connection so all purchases were cash only. Sarah had thirty dollars meaning she had to be careful about her purchases, since it might be some time before she could get more money from the bank or that bank and credit cards would work again. She'd have to live on pasta and the like for a while. She could hear the generators running to keep some of the freezers and coolers working. There was no bread, eggs, or meat, and many of the dry goods were gone as well. Toilet paper and paper towels apparently were the first things to be sold out. All the shelves would soon be empty. Then what would people do?

Operation salvage at her house was more difficult than she imagined it would be. She started at the garage end thinking that might be the easiest way to get to the basement and her mountain bike, which she had left there. Using just her hands, and her own strength, she was able to dismantle enough of the roof to see that the area below ground level was full of water, as if the roof had fallen on a swimming pool. The tsunami had obviously reached to the house, but this house must have been bolted to its foundation, unlike many she had seen, for everything was stacked on top of the cement walls of the foundation of the basement. Sarah now realized she needed tools like a reciprocating saw, hammer, and crow bar if she was going to be able to find anything. She gave up for the moment wondering how she could get the use of any tools, and how she would get rid of the nearly four feet of sea water filling what was left of the basement.

-10-

For three days Sarah picked away at the edges of the wreckage of her home piling the pieces she removed down near the road. A metal pipe that had been the power mast to the house served as her makeshift crow bar allowing her to finally expose the doorway from the garage to the basement. She felt like she was being drawn by a mystical force to get through that opening and she would discover all sorts of useful stuff beyond where the now missing door had been.

Mother Nature continued to visit each night talking about how earth needed to be treated as a single being. That humans were connected to the web of life like everything else. When one part of the web was disturbed, the whole web was affected and humans had interfered with all webs on the planet without learning the lesson of the sacred balance of nature. Like Sarah's own inner voice, she was starting to get, well, annoying, and Sarah wished she would just let her sleep. Sarah already knew Mother Nature was correct.

The excavator was in front of her place again. The operator had turned the engine off. and was clambering off, so

Sarah walked down towards him to see what was going on. Once on the ground he walked up towards her, "Hi. I'm Cal. I see you working on your place and wondered if you wanted me to move some of the bigger stuff for you?" Cal was a skookum man with thinning blonde hair and a large gut hanging over his belt.

"That would be fantastic! I'm Sarah. This was my parents' house. I was away when the quake happened. Come up and see what you think." It was a slight grade up about ten feet from the road.

Standing at the side of the garage Cal said, "I could use the bucket to dig a hole to drain that water. Next I could push all the joists and roof to the other end if that helps you?"

"Would it ever! I have no way of paying you though."

"Don't worry. They have us logging our hours promising us it will come out of some emergency fund. We met the Prime Minister and Premier yesterday. We've cleared most of the roads, stopped all the gas leaks and fires, and now we are supposed to make sure no more structures collapse. You know, for safety reasons. I have watched you for a coupla' days now. This is the least I can do."

Cal had his Komatsu in position in no time and started to knock a small hole in the foundation to drain the water down the hill at the side of the house. A few shovels made a trench speeding the release of the water. The Murrays joined Sarah to watch the action. Several other passersby stopped to watch as well. Five minutes later Cal moved the machine closer so that he could start moving the roof away from where Sarah stood and towards the other side of the property. She couldn't help but be impressed with his skill at delicately moving things with such a large piece of equipment. And then she saw something she never expected.

Running in front of the excavator so Cal would have to see her, frantically waving her arms, she got him to stop and emerge from his cab, "Cal, it's my dad! You've got to help me."

Cal could now see what she was looking at, and jumped down to get in front of her. Turning to the Murrays, he said, "Sir, I need you to help me. Ma'am, you need to take Sarah away from here."

It was too late, Sarah was sobbing uncontrollably, and had fallen to her knees. Mrs. Murray was comforting her as she had before. Both arms around Sarah while whispering calming words in her ear.

The two men climbed down into the former basement and were joined by three of the onlookers. They had found the rotting putrid bodies of Sarah's mom and dad. They wrapped them in wet carpets found on the floor. Two of the men lost their last meal and they all had to cover their noses due to the smell. Word of the discovery spread fast. A city truck pulled in front of the house to remove the latest quake statistics. Sarah collected herself in time to go to the truck and say her goodbyes, even though Cal told her not to look inside the carpets. A pall of silence fell over everyone regardless of this scene being repeated many times every day since the quake. Sarah was given a sheet of paper acknowledging what had been removed from the site. She was told to present it tomorrow at the arena somewhere, but she didn't really hear what they told her to do.

Slowly the onlookers moved on leaving only Cal and the Murrays with Sarah. Cal climbed back into the cab of the Komatsu to finish what he had started. Sarah thought he must have seen horrific things like this for days now. Perhaps he was as numb to it all as she felt at the moment. She watched, devoid of emotion, as he spent only a few more minutes to complete the job. Without even looking back at her he lifted the arm and bucket into neutral positions, turned the machine around and drove it back to the road. With a quick wave like he was Santa Claus he went back down Dallas Road to where he had come from. Sarah wondered if PTSD would be a problem for Cal when all of this was over. Would it be a problem for all the quake survivors?

Sarah didn't know what or how to feel. She only knew she wanted to be alone. She thanked the Murrays, excused herself and went to lay down in her tent. It was a mystery to her why she had reacted the way she had because she had suspected the worst outcome for her parents even before she got back to Victoria. When she hadn't found them the hope they had somehow survived and gone elsewhere dominated her mind. She had hoped that perhaps after her kayak trip she could form a more adult relationship with both of them. Now she had another whole set of problems to deal with.

Her body filled with restless energy so she decided to go for a walk to clear her head. Tomorrow she'd go back to the arena and sort out what needed to be done. Today she would just walk to find a good vantage point and stare out to sea until she felt better. A long walk would allow the angst to leave her body one footstep at a time.

Sitting on a rock shelf at Clover Point, Sarah was able to calm her emotions, and begin reflecting on her parents. She realized that she hardly knew her father who had really never done much with or for her. He just gave orders and did his own thing. Lived in his own world where children were just an inconvenience. Sarah was much closer to her mother, but didn't feel a strong connection there either. Her parents were just cold people. Strange how after such a short time she felt closer to Sam and Pete than to her own parents. According to her inner voice that's the way it was. She'd never even find out why they were so cold towards her. And actually to each other as well. Was it a generational thing?

-11-

A month later Sarah was still living in her tent on her family's land. She had managed to salvage more than she expected from the remains of the house, including the will from her parents safe. As she expected she was named to be the beneficiary to the house, but she was experiencing difficulties in getting all the legal ducks to line up because there were so many people in the same situation as her.

She had built a rough structure over and around her tent that included a bit of a kitchen area that was out of the rain. Sarah still cooked on her camp stove. Food supply chains were slowly returning to normal, but she was hesitant to buy too much as she had to store extras outside, and had had her belongings stolen several times. It was better just to shop every day.

Getting the house rebuilt with the insurance her parents took out was following the same pattern as her inheritance. Two steps forward followed by two steps back. After a month so many people were frustrated that the federal government was getting involved to force the hand of the insurance companies. They also had come through with grants and loans to allow people to get started rebuilding. None of which would apply to Sarah until her inheritance was finalized. Sometimes it appeared whatever bureaucrat she dealt with didn't take her seriously because of her age. Twenty-five year old people just didn't usually own property on Dallas Road. Legally Sarah didn't own it yet.

Her daily routine of going to see bureaucrats and do her food shopping only furthered her growing frustration. It didn't help that next door the Murray house was already being rebuilt albeit slowly due to a lack of tradesmen. Each day another brick of anger was added to the wall of frustration she felt growing inside her. At least the vision of Mother Nature had quit lecturing her every night. Going for long walks and riding her bike around Victoria helped dissipate the tension somewhat. Nevertheless, it continued to grow inside her until she felt she might burst. It was constant work on her part to be civil with the people she had to deal with every day. Her inner voice told her she should be proud of how she was conducting herself in these trying times. If only she could talk with Sam and Pete around the campfire.

Sarah had tried to contact Sam and Pete, but the infrastructure was still not back together enough yet. She even thought of kayaking up to the Comox Valley to see them. Or trying to get on a ship heading that way. Road works were supposedly going quicker than expected, so maybe she would be able to go by road soon. Besides, she had to stay in Victoria to sort everything out. And inevidably, her days went by.

-12-

Walking back from getting food for dinner that night Sarah became aware that there were three young men following her. The day was one of those overcast West Coast days with little air movement and a light 'Scotch mist' falling. She had her hood up over her head to keep dry. So did the three following her. She was sure she'd seen them before around the area. They looked to be about eighteen years old and always seemed to be together. One was taller and darker than the two smaller, lighter ones. She always felt like the two smaller ones were like puppy dogs following the taller boy. They followed her right to her house, so she kept walking. She didn't know why, but decided to walk around the long block past her house to see what they'd do.

Sarah felt foolish losing her tail like this, but they had followed her for about ten blocks involving several turns. When she went north on Government she felt relieved to see them continue east along Dallas. She continued around the block anyways.

Dinner that night was a chicken stir fry on rice with an orange/ginger sauce from Thrifty's she had never tried before. She went to bed satisfied with her dinner, however she still felt weird about her reaction to the three young men who had walked behind her. It took her a long time to go to sleep thinking about all the things she needed to do and how her day had ended.

The tent zipper noisily flying open woke her from a deep sleep. Before she could say or do anything two strong hands had her ankles and she was being pulled out of her tent feet first. She couldn't really see who was holding her but she yelled, "What're you doing? Let go of me!"

A gruff muffled voice said, "Get her out of the bag. Pull her out to the open."

Sarah was kicking and struggling as best she could, quickly realizing there was three of them. "Fuck off, bastards!", she screamed just before duct tape was put over her mouth. Once they had her out of the bag, one on each side of her held an arm with one hand and pulled her legs apart holding her ankles with the other hand. She could see they all wore black balaclavas and she knew what was going to happen next.

She always thought she'd panic in a situation like this. Surprisingly she felt calm despite the adrenalin coursing through her veins. As she felt her panties and shirt ripped off her she told herself this wasn't going to happen. As the third one got on top of her trying to thrust his penis inside her she had a spasm of strength that got her right hand free from the left hand of the smaller one holding that side. In a flash she had her hand between her legs and grabbed the scrotum of the turd on top of her. She twisted hard, felt his alcohol breathe scream in her face, and scraped her nails along his penis as he pulled away.

With one of their group lying on the grass writhing in pain, the other two released Sarah to come to his aid, but not before administering a barrage of kicks and curses at Sarah. Covering her head to protect herself she was still aware of a flashlight coming from the Murrays. She could hear the villains scurrying away and Mr. Murray yelling at them and chasing them towards the street.

"Sarah, you alright?" He was back at her side.

The flashlight in her face brought Sarah back to reality. She shielded her eyes and started to assess how she was. She realized she was sobbing and that her ribs hurt with each sob and breathe. Her head was fine as were her legs, but both arms hurt from blocking kicks. "I don't know", was all she could get out. She realized she was naked. Mr. Murray put her nearby sleeping bag on her with as much care as he could.

"Don't move. I'll get help and the misses." And off he went.

Sarah laid there curled in a ball thinking about where did he think she would go?

In seconds flat Mrs. Murray was there mothering her and checking her injuries. A huge bruise was forming on her side and Mrs. Murray was convinced Sarah had broken ribs and a broken wrist. As time went on, and the adrenalin subsided, it did hurt like hell.

"Did they rape you?"

"One tried…, but I got an adrenalin rush and stopped him. The other two were holding me. I'm stronger than the littlest one and broke my hand free and hurt the privates of the rapist one."

"You are so brave, Sarah. The ambulance is coming now." They could hear the siren approaching quickly.

Sarah had stopped crying, and just felt sick and violated. "Why me?", was all she could think to say. Over and over again between groans of pain.

There were two paramedics from the ambulance. Sarah knew it shouldn't matter, but she was glad one was a young woman about her age. They splinted her forearm and stretchered her down to the ambulance under what felt like a great weight of blankets to warm her up. She realized that she had started to shiver. Was it shock settling in or just the down following the adrenalin rush?

At Victoria General the nurses efficiently got her settled, while they waited for the doctor to see to her injuries. A female policewoman appeared and started to question her taking copious notes as she did so. When she heard a bit of Sarah's story she said this was one of a series of rapes reported since the earthquake. Sarah told Officer Giles that she had damaged the scrotum of the rapist before he'd got in her. And she showed her the nails on her right hand being sure she had evidence under them. She had always been able to grow long strong fingernails just like her mom. Giles took samples under her fingers and along her thighs carefully explaining everything she was doing.

Officer Giles was just finishing when the doctor arrived. Giles started to explain the situation, but the doctor wanted to hear it all from Sarah. She was already tired of telling the sequence of events knowing she'd have to tell it many more times yet. Checking her over the doctor noted boot tread marks on her side and made sure that Giles saw them. By now she had a photographer with her and Sarah gave them permission to photograph her injuries. At her genitals Sarah was surprised to learn that her pubic area was bruised and that he had got to the front of her vagina inflaming that area as well. At the time she had not felt that at all.

Sarah asked all in the room, "How can a man have an erection in that situation? It's hardly romantic. It's a violent subjugation of another."

Giles said, "I've never understood that either. The control of another is what excites them."

"I guess. It still doesn't make much sense."

"I know Sarah. Listen, is it ok if I get a formal statement from you tomorrow and we go after these delinquents, because they have to be stopped?"

"Yes. I'll press charges. I think I know who did this. They followed me earlier in the day."

"OK. I suspect you'll be here tomorrow, so I'll see you in the morning. Hope you feel better."

The doctor insisted on x-rays for her ribs and left arm finding fractures in both. He also insisted she be held overnight at least, which suited Sarah because she didn't feel like moving anywhere. Sleeping in her tent no longer appeared to be a good idea. Especially not until these evil men were behind bars.

-13-

She didn't feel better the next day. Her torso hurt at the slightest movement. It even hurt to talk or take a decent sized breath. Her arm was in a cast but throbbed relentlessly. Getting up to pee was excruciating, but there was no way she was using a diaper or bed pan. After a breakfast of coffee, toast, and some weird porridge, Sarah fell back asleep.

"Sarah, time to wake up."

What? Where was she?

It was a nurse standing over her, "The doctor is here with a policewoman".

Remembering the answer to all her questions Sarah struggled to sit up higher. The doctor told her to stay as she was. Constable Giles stood in the background waiting her turn.

"How's your pain this morning?", the doctor asked like it was part of a standard sequence he had to follow.

"I hurt all over when I move or breathe. Probably worse than yesterday."

"We will look after that. I need to check you all over to make sure there isn't more we need to look for. Are you ok if the constable observes for her investigation?"

Groggily Sarah gave her consent even though she just wanted to be left alone to curl back up into the fetal position. The doctor was gentle but still caused her to gasp periodically as he turned her this way and that. He kept the poking to a minimum letting out a couple of "humphs" as he observed her condition. Several times he pointed things out to the constable and pictures were taken.

"Alright Sarah?" He said it like a question, so she nodded. "You have some massive contusions, particularly around your back and ribs. We need to confirm there is no internal bleeding and I want to see the condition of your spleen and kidneys. We may as well keep you here until we have done all the tests and scans. Besides, you don't look like you are going anywhere very fast right now, and we have space for you. OK with all that?"

"Yes, I understand. Besides, I'm living in a tent at the moment so this is definitely better. I'm not sure I'd feel safe out there anymore anyway."

Giles explained, "She is on the property of her family home which was destroyed by the quake and tsunami." To Sarah, "We processed the site early this morning and got some more evidence. We think two of them may have returned and ransacked things before running off. Probably scared off by your neighbor, uh, a Mr. Murray who we took a statement from. Their boot prints matched those we suspect from last night, that are on your side, so we're pretty sure it's the same men."

The doctor was writing on his clipboard this whole time only looking up when Giles finished. "In that case I've ordered you to stay put for at least two more days. Right, I'll leave you with the nurse and constable and arrange this scan which should happen soon." He left the room like a person with a lot on his plate.

Constable Giles then took Sarah's official statement doing the writing for her. Several times they had to stop because Sarah had the whole horrible event come flashing back to her. With the doctor she had felt coldly removed from it all. Now it was all too real again, as if it was happening right then. All the panic, anger, violation and pain washed over her like a wave. At the end Giles read the whole thing back and Sarah signed it, careful not to make any fast movements, knowing she hadn't actually taken in much of what Giles had been reading.

"Sarah, before I leave I want you to know how seriously we are pursuing this. I have already been told the DNA evidence we got off you will all be viable and should lead to a conviction on its own. But we have much more evidence. The DNA processessing has been pushed forward and we could well have the perpetrators on file and make an arrest in short order."

"Thanks. Sorry about losing it a bit there. It all came back. I hope that doesn't happen when this goes to court. Not looking forward to that."

"We will support you in that, Sarah. I don't remember if I told you that these three have done this at least a half dozen other times that have been reported. You won't be alone even though you can't contact, or even know about, the others."

Sarah nodded and thanked Giles again just as two strapping large orderlies pushed a bed into the room. After confirming her name and date of birth they carefully moved her to the new bed on wheels to take her away for her scans.

The doctor from the morning was there with the technician to assess the images and reassure Sarah that she had no internal bleeding. Other than the broken ribs she should make a speedy recovery due to her age and fitness level. Sarah wasn't so sure. Physically she felt like a truck had run over her. Mentally she felt very fragile and frightened. A male nurse had come to check on her. She recoiled from him, and started crying. She was embarrassed that she now lost control so easily. Perhaps it was more than the rape. It was all that had occurred over the past few weeks. The Wave. Sam and Pete. Her parents. The house. Now this on top of it all made her feel like a mess inside her head. It was all swirling around and around like a pinwheel. Even her inner critic was confused and out of sorts.

After two days Sarah found that her brain was no longer mush. She was actually starting to think about what she'd do next when the medical staff had decided she could go back home. She had doubts about being able to cope with living as she had, however, needs must. She found her anger hadn't changed. Her coping mechanisms seemed to be evolving, trying to make herself as invisible as she could. She talked softly and only as much as was necessary. All her clothes had become evidence or ruined so the kind Murrays had gone through her stuff and brought her some baggy neutral coloured clothes from her belongings. Her biggest dilemma was what to do about her hair? Talking to her day nurse she decided not to cut it all off. Sarah was going to use it to help her hide from the world by wearing it down and half covering her face under her bowed head. She might not bother with a pony tail any more.

She was released from hospital just before noon. Sarah took a bus downtown getting off at Douglas and Fort. She walked gingerly to the lawyer's office where she had been instructed to take her parents' will to see if any progress had been made. If nothing else perhaps she could get some money out of the savings she knew her parents had had. If only her body didn't hurt so much.

The office of Slater, Thompson, and Sihota was on the second floor. Sarah took the stairs fearing the elevator might feel too claustrophobic. Half way up the stairs her pain was too great causing her to stop to rest with her hyper-vigilant inner critic chastising her for not using the lift. The office was classily set up with original artwork on the walls and leather chairs for the clients. The legal assistant that greeted Sarah looked like a model dressed ready for the runway. She was tall and slim, dressed in a form fitting green dress that highlighted her figure. Her British accent made her seem even more classy. Her looks and voice reminded Sarah of Kate Middleton. There was a definite aura about her that Sarah couldn't put her finger on. Her gold embossed name tag said Bryony.

The whole ambience made Sarah feel more intimidated than she normally would have. Her self-confidence shot, she wanted to leave. Somehow the nice legal secretary made her explain why she was there without an appointment. Sarah was now visibly shaking causing Bryony to glide around her desk, place an arm around Sarah, and usher her into an empty conference room. "It's alright love. I'll get Mr. Sihota straight away. First, I'll get you something to drink."

Bryony returned in no time with a tray that had tea, coffee, and shortbreads on it. "There, there, love. Take some big breathes and help yourself to whatever you want. Sarah, Mr. Sihota has been trying to contact you. We are nearly finished with your file. I completed the report several days ago." With that, she turned on her high heels and appeared to float out of the room. Her presence and manner helped calm Sarah down. Or was it her smell that lingered in the room?

After one sip of her tea Sarah was brought back to reality by the entrance of Mr. Sihota. He was as disheveled as Bryony had been perfect. Sihota reminded Sarah of Colombo with his stained suit jacket that didn't match his pants, socks, or shoes. He had two files under his arm which he managed to spill all over the table while trying to shake Sarah's hand in introduction. Out of nowhere Bryony's perfect hands and nails arrived to put everything back in order in less time than Mr. Sihota had taken to mess them all up. Sarah could only think this had happened before.

"Bryony, could you stay?" To Sarah he said, "She'll make this all go smoother".

"Let me get Heather to man the front desk. I'll be back sharpish." Sarah could tell that it was Bryony who really ran this office.

Sihota started without his assistant, immediately getting things muddled up due to starting with the wrong papers. Those hands were back again giving him things in the correct order. The rest of the meeting ran like clockwork. After going through all the things they had done Sihota was able to conclude the proceedings rather well without any sign of his earlier bumbling approach. Then Sarah noticed he was mostly reading from a sheet probably prepared by his incredible legal assistant.

"The upshot of all this, Sarah, is that you are the only and last survivor of the estate, and so it all goes to you. The four houses, the car collection and garage, the stocks, and the three bank accounts. All the information is in here. You have to take this to the Royal Bank and get the accounts changed to your name which has already been requested so it should only take a few days. Only the house on Dallas Road was destroyed. Two of the others have renters. The monthly rents go into the third account at the Royal. The fourth house was being renovated when the quake hit so it is unoccupied at the moment. They have all been approved for habitation in the post-quake assessments. We will have to work on the shares for a bit as they are all over the place. In fact we still might not have them all! Any questions?"

Sarah knew she looked a sight. Now she was totally shocked as well. She realized her mouth was open and she was shaking slightly. Couldn't think of what to say. All was finally revealed to her that this was what her dad was always so preoccupied about. "I...I had no idea they had all this. I thought putting me through UVIC put them in the poor house."

"You are not poor any more young lady. Listen, I have an appointment waiting. Can you contact Bryony if you need more information, but please make appointments to see me in the future."

Sarah painfully rose to shake his hand as he left, and then slumped back into her chair. Bryony had organized all the papers she needed. She passed them to Sarah with a smile. "On the top of that file you'll find a sheet outlining everything you need to do. I've ordered them logically, but you don't need to follow my directions. I've included ten death cert's for each parent. You'll need them at the bank and to take possession of things. I can do more for you when and if you need. At the back is our fee breakdown which is already removed from the inheritance. You owe us nothing additional. Simple as. With all due respect, love, you don't look well."

That was all Sarah needed to break into tears. With Bryony hugging her and brushing her hair back from her face she settled quickly. "Sorry, I've only today been released from hospital."

"Not simply your arm then? What were you in there for? If I can be so bold to ask?"

"No worries. I was attacked. Four days ago."

"Oh love! I'm so sorry for you. Contact me if you need help at all. For anything."

"Bryony, you've done so much already. I can't thank you enough."

"It's my job, love. How will you get home? Let me call you a cab."

"No, it's ok. Besides, I don't have enough for a cab right now."

"Sarah, are you in that tent on Dallas?"

"Yah, I..."

"No, you are coming home with me. We've a spare room. Simple as. And we live in Fernwood near to one of your inherited properties."

"Bryony, this is so kind, way past the reach of your job here."

"Also love, we need to set up an appointment for you at the Royal to sort out your financials. I'll do that right now. I have a contact. You'll love her." She already had her cellphone to her ear quickly making an appointment for thirty minutes later. "Ok. Jo is expecting you with all your info you've got in the folder. The bank is three blocks from here. You go do your banking and I'll finish up here and we'll meet back here and go to our place for dinner. You are definitely staying at ours until we get you sorted. Got it?"

"Can we go by mine to pick up some things first?"

Bryony thought that was no problem and insisted on riding the elevator down with Sarah to make sure she got headed in the right direction to get to the bank on time. Sarah used the money she had left to buy a latte and a scone, which she ate while shuffling along to the bank, with her cast held so her hand was in the air to stop the throbbing.

Jo was waiting for her inside the entrance. "You must be Sarah, I'm Jo. Bryony told me to expect ...well you." Jo was as strikingly beautiful as Bryony. She had long blonde hair and wore a bright red pant suit topped off with matching red lipstick and nails. "Come with me to my office."

Jo already had the three accounts up on her computer, and a pile of paperwork for Sarah to sign once she had turned over the required documents. Jo explained that Sarah couldn't access the accounts for three more working days, but then they were hers. A checking account with several thousand in it, a savings account with several hundred thousand in it, and the rental account again with several hundred thousand in it. Sarah had never seen accounts with so much money in them. Jo also explained that the Royal had some of the investments her father had made that would come to her as soon as the lawyers had it all sorted out. "Want to see it? But don't tell B. that I showed you."

"OK." Sarah was sensing a lot of familiarity between Jo and Bryony. She gasped when Jo showed her that her dad had over a million invested here alone.

"You can't tell B. that I showed you. She'd kill me. When we get the go ahead from her I'll call you in and we'll spend some time going through this portfolio. Most of it is in longer term stuff we can't change right now, but we could play with some of it if you want..." Jo was interrupted by a light knock on the door.

The door opened before Jo could say anything and in came Bryony. Jo rose and gave her a kiss on the lips and held her hand. Turning towards Sarah, Jo explained, "This is my wife, Bryony. I am glad you are coming home with us. I have a huge stew in the croc pot that we couldn't eat on our own."

Not for the first time today Sarah found herself speechless.

Bryony said, "You two finished? I have the car illegally parked. See you back at the chateau, darling." She gave Jo a peck on the cheek as she helped Sarah to her feet. Making sure she had all the papers in order, again, she then lead her by the elbow of her broken arm to the waiting BMW.

At the Dallas Road property Bryony was shocked that Sarah was living in the conditions she saw. "Sarah, you must gather everything of value from here. You are not coming back to live like a squatter as long as I have anything to say about it. Let's load my car up, and you can stay at our place until... well whenever. Love, this is not conducive to you recovering from what you've been through." Sarah was too knackered to argue and so she told Bryony what needed to move to the car while she went through her stuff trying to find enough decent looking clothes to kind of fit in with her hosts.

-14-

Dinner with Bryony and Jo was the most relaxing time Sarah had experienced since the quake. She almost forgot why she was there, until she moved to get up and her ribs reminded her. Her hosts occupied the ground floor and basement of a totally renovated three floor 1920's house on Gladstone in Fernwood. They rented out the two flats above them to mature UVIC students. Sarah was given her own bedroom and bathroom as the other two had an ensuite and huge walk in closet off their room.

Both Bryony and Jo changed into t-shirts and old sweat-pants as soon as they got home. Without the clothes and make-up Sarah could see they were both probably around forty years old. Seeing them like this further helped her relax and not feel so inadequate around them. As the wine flowed, Sarah told them about her kayak trip, the freighter rescue, and how she survived the tsunami and got back to Victoria. Eventually they quizzed her so much she told them about her sexual assault, causing a shocked silence after Bryony and Jo expressed how sad they were that she'd had to go through this ordeal.

"Listen love, talking about this will be painful but probably also helpful. Anything Jo or I can do to assist your healing journey you just let us know."

Jo said angrily, "I hope they get the pricks. I feel like we should ... no that wouldn't help."

"No Jo. That is not what we'll do to help. Right now though, love, I'm going to pour the best bubble bath you ever had. Tidy." And Bryony was off to fill the tub.

Sarah felt she couldn't say no to this offer but knew she needed help getting the bandages off and then replaced afterwards. In the bathroom she told Bryony about her dilemma and that she'd probably get some blood on the towel when drying. Bryony told her not to worry, they had lots of towels. As Sarah started to undress Bryony let out an audible gasp when she saw the extent of the bruising and scrapes around Sarah's torso. When all the bandages were off she whispered, "Love, we shouldn't let Jo see you like this. She could just as well go after those guys straight away and I wouldn't bet against her."

"Wouldn't bet against me what?" Jo was at the door and saw the naked Sarah getting into the tub. "Holy shit! Those bastards! Sarah, nobody deserves what you got. I.. I.."

Bryony put her arm on Jo to try to calm her. "Let's let Sarah enjoy the bath and get us another glass of that Pinotage." As the door closed Sarah sunk down into the water soaking as much strength from it as she could.

Jo came in ten minutes later, "Sorry about earlier Sarah. I've decided not to kill those wankers. Let the courts do their worst B. says and I guess I agree. I was a nurse in my twenties so I can fix your new dressings. Just call when you need me. Tomorrow, B. and I have both taken the afternoon off and we'll give you a spa day, then go out to the pub for dinner. What do you say?"

"I say you two are incredible. How could I say no to an offer like that. I've never had a spa treatment."

"You won't regret it. Want some more wine?"

Sarah felt relaxed but drained of energy after the bath. Jo had done a stellar job with the polysporin and bandages. She definitely felt better than she had since the assault.

Bryony poured more wine from the third bottle on the table and switched the conversation to tomorrow. "Sarah, I know I've been bossing you about today, love, but, and tell me if I'm over stepping the mark, one of your inherited houses is in the next block. It's the one they had renovated and we've not seen anyone around there recently, so maybe they are finished. Since you have the keys why don't you check it out in the morning?"

Jo chimed in, "After you sleep in that is." They all laughed.

"That hurts." Sarah held her ribs still laughing. "Isn't laughter supposed to be the best medicine? Then why does it hurt so much?" When they'd all finished laughing she said, "Sounds like a great plan for tomorrow. Listen, I'll never be able to repay or thank you two enough. This has been wonderful and before today you didn't even know who I was. I mean, why did you decide to help me out so much?"

"Because it's the right thing to do, love. Simple as. Besides, I did know a fair lot about you. Don't tell Sihota. He'll say I've broken client confidentiality."

"Bryony, I'm so glad you did. I'm knackered and off to bed. 'Night you two."

Sarah had no dreams that night and only woke in the morning when the front door closed and locked because it was near her bedroom. The sadness was still there inside her. Perhaps it was buried a little deeper now. And maybe it would get more buried with each passing day. The anger was still as fresh as ever. She felt her emotions were still far too close to the surface. Today she had a mission to accomplish and thanks to Bryony and Jo her whole day was planned out and had her thinking ahead rather than being stuck in the present in a mire of pain and anger.

Jo had left her a note about breakfast. A house key laid on the bottom of the note. Those two were like the best. And she hadn't known them for twenty-four hours yet. A look at the microwave clock as she warmed up her coffee told her she had plenty of time. It was barely past eight. As she sipped her coffee she spent more time in her folder, researching her inheritance. She needed a lot more time to process what she'd learned yesterday. Nobody had said it, but she was now worth millions! She felt bad about how she had classified her father in the past. He had sure looked after her future!

Two hours later Sarah had finished going through the folder, and she had drained the coffee pot that had been left for her. Time to dress and check out the Gladstone property.

The house struck her with how big it was. It was three stories with balconies on each floor. Large solid wooden doors and leaded glass windows were about all that was left from the original materials. Everything else had been upgraded. A truck was in the driveway and two men were working on the gutters and fascia. "Just finishing the job off, ma'am. You are awful young to own a place like this, eh?"

Sarah thought the same. There was no way she was going to let him see any vulnerability in her though. "What's too young?" He mumbled something she didn't catch, leaving the impression that he realized he'd crossed the line. "I'm just going in to check on a few things."

"It's all finished and paid for, ma'am. We were short of materials to finish this side. We'll be done in an hour, and we'll be out of your hair."

"Thanks." What was her hair like? Probably all over the place. She hadn't been looking after it much for months.

Inside, the house was immaculate and seemed huge with no furniture in it. Her footfalls echoed under the twelve foot high ceilings. The kitchen and bathrooms were all redone with granite counters and new fixtures. Sarah expected the top two floors to be set up as rental units, but there was only one set of keys and the stairs were inside. She followed them up to find two more bathrooms and four more bedrooms. It was made for a large family. What would she do with it she wondered. The idea came to her that she could live here. It would be fun to furnish it. Keeping busy would keep her mind off thinking about her recent past.

Behind the house was a long garage with four doors. This had to be her dad's car collection. Searching the keys, as expected, she found one marked 'G'. There was a side door that it opened noisily. Those hinges needed oiling she thought as she found the light switches, and the four garage door openers. With all this light she was dazzled by the bright shiny perfectly preserved cars. She realized she had seen the Firebird and Mustang before. Had even ridden in them about a decade ago. There were seven of them carefully crammed in there. The two at the far end were under custom made covers. Sarah pulled each back enough to see the classic car plates. A 1928 Studebaker Erskine and a 1930 Buick. All this meant little to her. She only knew there was a small fortunes worth of antique cars here. More confusion about her dad clouded her head as she carefully closed up and locked the garage. Another thing to figure out what to do about.

Bryony and Jo had just then pulled up to their place in the BMW as Sarah got back there. "How's the pain today? Ready for your spa day?" Jo greeted her with a hug and kiss as did Bryony.

"Getting better daily. Last night sure helped. Will the spa day be better than that?"

Bryony enthused, "'Course it will, love! Unfortunately, we can't give you the full massage today. Jo says we have to be careful. But we'll do your unbruised parts."

"And your hair and nails and facial...the whole shebang. You'll be a brand new gal going out tonight." Jo was really into it.

Spa day involved the whole afternoon with Bryony and Jo taking turns, and doing each other as well. Sarah was reminded of when she was a young girl doing up dolls, not that she'd done it much. This time she was the doll. These two took pride in how they looked obviously doing this regularly. At the end Sarah was allowed to look in the mirror. She hardly recognized herself. For one thing, she'd never worn this much make-up or had her hair so curled and primped. The other two also had more make-up than they did for work. Apparently, this was the look for going out to dinner. A new experience for Sarah. Bryony was about the same size as Sarah so she was given a short dress and heals to wear to show off her new shiny smooth legs. The other two dressed even more provocatively.

The pub in the Fernwood Inn at the end of the street was classy, but it was a pub. When they walked in Sarah was aware of all eyes and heads turning their way and staying locked onto them even after they sat down in the most visible table right in the middle of the main room. Bryony and Jo carried on as if nothing was different. Sarah thought she could almost see the sensual aura of attraction glowing around these two beauties. She didn't feel like she was part of the aura, although it did put a smile on her face. Nevertheless, Sarah felt uncomfortably awkward. She tried not to let it show. She was also aware the cast on her arm made her different from the other two.

The male waiter was at their table as soon as they were seated. Sarah watched with amusement as Jo noticeably was hitting on the poor guy. After they'd ordered food Bryony was sitting on an old friends' lap in the far corner, while Jo had the poor waiter on a string. These two knew how to stir the pot using their looks and charms. Sarah had never seen anything like it and could only laugh inside. They were married. To each other. Obviously, nobody here knew that other than her, and she found it all very strange and amusing at the same time. The other thing Sarah noticed was that both Jo and Bryony had a lot to drink just like last night. She couldn't keep up and wasn't about to try.

Several hours later the three of them walked the few blocks home as if none of the previous hours had even happened. Jo declared it the perfect spa day and disappeared to bed with Bryony and Sarah following shortly after.

At breakfast the following morning, Sarah got stuck in to her granola and waited for Bryony and Jo to get settled before asking the question that had been on her mind before she fell asleep. "OK, you two. What was that all about last night?"

They stopped chewing and looked at each other. Jo nodded slightly. Bryony took a deep breath, "Vow of silence, love. We weren't going to tell anyone. Here goes. Jo and I are both in our late thirties and the call of nature has got us. We don't want to adopt and invitro seems wrong and expensive. We both want to have one kid."

Jo continued, "So we thought we simply have to find the right men to have casual sex with, don't tell anyone, get preggers and have a kid. Wham, bam, slam."

Sarah blurted out without thinking, "But you are both gay, and married."

"Don't think the worst of us, love. We have been talking about this for years and last night was our first trial run, knowing we were not bringing anybody home that time. We wanted to see how it might all go and feel. I was married to a guy in England when I was eighteen."

"So was I. Only I was nineteen and it was in Victoria. So we've been with men and actually like men. It's just that we are in love with each other and will still be after all this is over."

Sarah was gobsmacked, so said nothing covering up by filling her mouth with granola.

"Jo and I know this is taking advantage of the men, love, but half of them don't want to raise kids anyway. We do, and we don't see a better way to achieve our goal."

Sarah felt she had to break the silence, "I get it. And no, I don't think any worse of you two. You'll be great parents. What if only one of you gets pregnant, eh?"

"We've talked about all the possibilities, love, and we're game to accept whatever happens. We've given ourselves a two year window. Can you keep our secret?"

"No worries."

"What will you do today, love?"

"Bryony, I'm back to the bank, the copshop, and then I will check out the other two rentals and introduce myself if anyone is home. I'm keeping the one here on Gladstone. Think I'll move in there and take my time rebuilding Dallas Road. Can't believe Dad didn't even owe money on any of these. If I keep renting the others I will have a steady income and could go back to school or whatever."

"Good luck, love. Tonight we are out on a double date so you are on your own."

-15-

Sarah, feeling stronger every day, was able to see both of her rentals before visiting the bank to find out all was in order now so that she could withdraw some cash. She went to the old Dutch Bakery on Fort St. to have a Rueben and soup just like she used to have with her mom from time to time. It was like time travelling back to the sixties inside the busy cafe part of the bakery with the booths and arborite table tops. The food was also 'old school', but delicious. She even recognized the waitress, a semi-gothic attired woman who looked like she didn't belong here, but judging by her rapoire with the clientele was much appreciated and even loved.

Constable Giles had arranged to meet with Sarah at two. Sarah arrived early even though she wasn't looking forward to this and Giles saw her immediately regardless. Inviting Sarah into an empty office she said, "Have a seat, Sarah. I'll get you a coffee."

When Giles returned, she opened a file and started in without looking at Sarah which seemed somewhat ominous. After describing their investigation, interviews, and DNA results Giles finally looked up and met Sarah's now worried gaze. "Sarah, we caught the three perps! The ringleader in the end had to go to the Royal Jubilee to get his privates looked at. You really got him. When we went to arrest him the other two were visiting him, so we had a rare three for one day." Giles had a big grin on her normally serious face. Sarah took notice of her for the first time particularly her big brown eyes and thick eyebrows. Previously Giles had just been a cop in a uniform.

"Hmph. So,... what happens now?" Sarah took a sip of the tepid bitter coffee wondering how to feel about this news. She should be elated but she felt dread, because now the slow-moving justice system would continue to dredge this all up for her repeatedly for who knew how long.

"They will be charged in court tomorrow. The crown prosecutor is outside waiting to talk to you so the whole process can begin. You need to know we have him on several other rapes as well. This scum will go down for a good long while once his infected testicles and pecker heal."

Sarah's emotional numbness was worsened by talking to the prosecutor. After three hours in the police station, she decided to head back to Gladstone, forgetting that Bryony and Jo would be there primping for their double date. Surprisingly there was a calculated calmness about both of them. They dressed much more conservatively this time, although Sarah still was aware of how strikingly beautiful they both were in different ways. She still didn't know how to feel about their unusual mission. Or about them in general. She knew not to be judgmental though, because they were so kind to her, and she was already feeling really close to them. There was such an honest sincerity about Bryony and Jo.

As the clock approached eight, Sarah decided to walk to the Fernwood Inn for a beer and burger and then go back to her inherited house on Gladstone to take inventory of what she needed to set it up to move in. The next day was Saturday so her immediate plan was to use some of her money to furnish the house .

Sarah woke early and could already hear noise in the kitchen and the low voices of both Bryony and Jo. She joined them for the pancake breakfast Jo had prepared. "So, ladies, how did the double date go?"

Bryony and Jo looked at each other apparently not knowing what to say. Jo broke the short-lived silence, "Well B. never got home 'till the wee hours. Mine was a bit weird and definitely won't work."

Sarah and Jo both turned their heads to look at Bryony. She struggled to get out, "Yeh. ...Well, this could already be it. We talked half the night away and he'll do the deed, I mean did do the deed in the end and I know I'm ovulating so I can only hope."

"Wow." Sarah couldn't say more.

Bryony felt like she had to tell more. "Get this. He's married and has a kid with his wife. They both sleep away from home, and he understands our predicament, and claims he won't be involved afterwards, unless I need him to."

"Lucky ducky. The double date was to help out his friend who I ended up with. He's a religious quack who couldn't handle us being married or any aspect of our little project.

So I'm back to the drawing board. I never had good luck with men. I think it's this cursed blonde hair."

"I'm so sorry, lover." Turning to Sarah, Bryony asked, "What are your plans for today, Sarah?"

"Well, I don't know how to tell you guys this. I've decided to move into the place on Gladstone. I really appreciate all you've done for me. I'll definitely stay in touch after I move. You two are wonderful. Oh, and today I'm going furniture shopping."

Jo instantly jumped to her feet. "That's so cool. You have to let us help. I've got so many good ideas...."

"Jo, sit down my lover. Sarah might want to do this on her own."

"No, I can use all the help I can get. Let's go shopping!"

And so it was decided, off they went with Bryony driving from warehouse to warehouse. Beds and couches from one place, dining room and kitchen stuff from another. At an art store Jo was admiring an original painting by local painter, Dana Statham, so Sarah bought it without telling them it was going to be her gift to them for helping her out in her time of need.

They had only purchased from places that delivered, which started on the Monday of the next week. By the end of the week Sarah, Bryony, and Jo had the place all set up and Friday was Sarah's move-in day. That night she hosted the Murrays and Bryony and Jo for dinner and her housewarming. She had no idea what Mr. and Mrs. Murray would think of her two new friends. She also knew at some point she'd offer the Murray's a room upstairs until their rebuild was complete.

-16-

Winter passed without much change in greater Victoria. The South Island remained cut off from the rest of the Island. Goods and services had to arrive via water which remained more difficult than it had been formerly because the rebuilding of the docks progressed at the same snail's pace as everything else. The Canadian Army had been brought in to assist with road and bridge reconstruction. Provincial and Federal Governments were doing all they could, bringing workers and construction companies from back east. Rumours were rampant about the rate of repairs. A persistent one had the Island Highway reopening in the Spring. Sarah had Sam and Pete's addresses and planned to head up Island as soon as the road opened. She had heard they had made it to Tofino, so it made sense that they had made it home. She had thought of phoning or writing Sam but the mail and phone had only recently started to reach normal service. Besides it would be more fun to simply show up and surprise them. She had to do something soon for they probably thought she was dead.

Sarah's new home was working out really well sharing with Mr. and Mrs. Murray. She couldn't think of them by their given names. Kenneth and Daphne often didn't even call each other by their names. It was Mom and Dad. And to Mrs. Murray Sarah was always, "Dearie".

Her Dallas Road property wouldn't be rebuilt for years, although somehow Mr. Murray had got their house started but it involved one delay after another. Presently only the foundation and drains were in place after the whole site had been levelled and the destroyed house removed.

Her health had returned quickly, and mentally she thought she was doing well, except that periodically unexpected events would bring a massive sadness over her, and she'd retreat inside herself and also physically disappear if she could. Fortunately, she was now recovering rapidly. Bryony and Jo really helped her in this area. The three of them spent a lot of time together. Bryony had got pregnant from that one encounter. Jo had not been so fortunate and now doubted if she could have sex with a man. Sarah had offered to pay for an invitro sperm donor procedure, which was now being considered. Jo claimed they had lots of money so that wasn't the issue. Sarah also wondered if she could be with a man again, realizing she didn't fancy women either. Bryony thought Sarah only needed more time. Still it was great to have these two to talk so openly about even the most personal of issues.

To give the Murrays more room, Sarah spent the night with Bryony and Jo about once a week. Bryony was five months pregnant now and starting to show. Jo claimed to be jealous of the healthy glow of her skin. Bryony complained that she had to wear dresses all the time now for comfort and to cover her condition up. Over dinner one Friday night after finishing the main course there was a knock on the door.

Jo was up in a flash, she had already assumed the role of Bryony's caregiver. "Who could that be?"

From the table the other two couldn't see or really hear the conversation at the door. There was no doubt it was a man talking with Jo. They only talked a couple of minutes when they heard the door click closed and Jo came back to the table with a bemused expression on her face.

"Who was that, lover?"

Jo smiled and said, "Your sperm donor wondering if his little swimmers might be needed again if they hadn't done the trick the last time. Ha ha."

"Well, I did tell him not to contact me again. That was the deal."

"B., how else would he know? You never told him."

"True enough, love. You know, Sarah cover your ears, his little swimmers are needed again. For you!"

Jo laughed nervously and looked away deep in thought. She got up and walked to study the Dana Statham hanging prominently in the dining room. She refilled her wine glass twice to make sure it was really full. "B., you think it would be ok for me to see him?"

"All brothers and sisters are genetically linked. Well, most of them. So how would this be any different? You should do it."

"Trouble is, kind woman, without you ovulating beside me I'm all over the place now."

And so it was decided that this was the route Jo would take. Sarah sat back saying nothing, watching these two wild spirits work their magic together. She'd heard of urban goddesses and here she was hanging out with two of them. That night a knock at the door had started the magic for Jo, and Sarah was sure she'd be pregnant soon and they would have their two desired kids.

-17-

It took eight months for the Inland Island Highway to be reopened and about eight minutes for Sarah to decide to take the Island Links bus up to the Comox Valley to finally do what she should have done long ago to see Sam and Pete to put their minds at rest that she had survived the tsunami as well.

The trip up Island was slow due to all the single lane bridges and roadworks that were still going on. At the Driftwood Mall in Courtenay Sarah flagged down a cab to take her out of town to Forbidden Plateau Road where she remembered they both lived. The cabbie looked up their names and soon had their addresses entered into his GPS. He was a young immigrant who spoke broken English, but was obviously clever and ambitious. His dark hair and skin and high bridged nose probably placed him as being of Middle Eastern origin. Sarah was afraid to ask. Besides, he talked the whole way and she couldn't get many words in anyways.

In ten minutes they were instructed to turn left and in, "A hundred yards turn left again. You will have reached your destination." Slowly the cab drove down the narrow lane through a thick fir and cedar forest to a small clearing where the driveway turned into a roundabout in front of the house. Then Sarah saw Sam and Pete coming towards the cab.

She was out of the cab before it fully stopped and hugged Pete so hard that she almost knocked him over. She felt how thin he'd become. She kissed him more than once and didn't realize she was crying until she felt his damp cheeks. Pete kept repeating, "Sarah, oh Sarah."

When she finally opened her eyes she realized it was Sam who had been stroking her back and probably holding her and Pete up. She let the old man go and hugged and kissed Sam the same way. "Sorry for the tears. I'm just so glad to see you two!"

"Us too. We didn't know what happened to you. We were able to find out you weren't listed as missing or ...you know. Dad was convinced you'd made it and we'd left Tofino too quickly for you to have time to get there."

"Truth is son, we had that one chance to possibly get back here so we took it." Turning to Sarah the old man continued, "We checked every way we could, Sarah but...". Sarah was hugging him again explaining how sorry she was that she hadn't got in touch earlier.

Pete said, "No apology needed. This surprise is better. I don't know if my heart can take more, let's go in for tea and crumpets."

Turning towards the house they realized the cabbie was still there. He stood sheepishly beside the car with Sarah's bag in his hands. Sarah thanked him profusely, apologized, and gave him a tip of more than double the fair. He climbed back in his cab with a big smile on his face.

Inside the house Pete crept to a chair and Sam prepared the tea. It was just like things had been on their kayak trip. Sarah felt so at home with these two men. Her adopted father and grandfather. That night she also met their wives and the wine flowed as they took turns explaining how their quake survival had gone. Pete only lasted until eight and shuffled off to bed with help from his wife, Jean.

Sarah turned to Sam with a questioning look that needed no words. He read her expression, "Sarah, he wouldn't tell you but the Big C really has returned aggressively. He's considered palliative now and has accepted that he is going to die at home. They gave him one to three months and that was four months ago. Stubborn old goat. The kayak trip seemed to slow the progression down and perhaps made the cancer go backwards. He was definitely better at the end than he was at the beginning."

Sarah enjoyed two days with Sam and Pete and their wives. They mostly stayed indoors, drank tea, ate, and told stories. Sarah explained about her inheritance but decided not to tell them about the sexual assault. Pete was really enthused about her dad's car collection. She couldn't answer all his questions about the details of the cars. She wished she had inspected them more closely in order to satisfy Pete's curiosity. Or taken pictures with her cellphone. She did tell them about the Murrays being in her new house with her. She also explained all about her new friends, Bryony and Jo. She told a bit of a fib about why she had to go back to Victoria the next day. She said she had an appointment with a lawyer. Which was kind of true only her appointment was actually the start of the court case.

-18-

Sarah was not really sure in her own mind why she was sitting in court at nine o'clock sharp waiting for the trial of her assaulter to begin. She was informed by the prosecutor that today would not involve her and all this was doing was to make her feel sad inside again, the victim all over again. Several other young women sat in her vicinity. Sarah suspected they were also his victims. There was much activity at the front of the court, people scurrying around with troubled expressions on their faces. The clerk and lawyers were called to the judge's chambers making Sarah think something was wrong. Bryony and Jo arrived together as all this was occurring. Bryony agreed that this was all a bit unusual, but it could involve the evidence or a juror or any number of things.

At 9:30 the court room was cleared with the explanation there would be no trial today. Bryony saw the prosecutor come into the large lobby, and went to him immediately to see what he could tell them. After a short guarded conversation Bryony returned to Sarah's side and said, "We've got to get out of here, love. I know a way out the side. I know that lawyer. There is going to be a press conference out front. You don't want to face the press. He hung himself in his cell moments before the trial."

"He ...what?" Sarah was completely taken aback.

Bryony grabbed her arm and turned her towards an emergency exit, "Come on love, we've got minutes to flee. We don't want them to see you." With Jo and Bryony flanking her they slid out the side of the courthouse getting away from the commotion on the front steps, unseen by the hungry media. Sarah had no idea a pregnant woman could move so quickly.

The BMW was illegally parked on a side street. Bryony was up to her usual parking mischief. She drove away from the courthouse in the opposite direction they needed to go to make sure they weren't seen. They would take the scenic albeit circuitous route to Fernwood.

Only with a coffee in hand sitting at the table on Gladstone did Bryony fully explain what she had found out. "Sarah, he hung himself without a note or anything. He used all the clothes he was given to dress in for court. Apparently, he had repeatedly told his lawyer that he didn't want to go to jail. He'd heard what the other inmates do to people like him. He couldn't face it so he took another coward's option."

"Hmm...what happens now?"

"Obviously there will not be a trial for that bastard."

Sarah didn't know what to think other than perhaps the ordeal was perhaps over. But would it ever be over for her? Rapist got what he...no Sarah don't let the anger win. "Bryony, what about the other two?"

"He didn't say, love. And I didn't think to ask."

Jo had been silent this whole time, "Let's celebrate with lunch down at the Fernwood. I'm buying."

"It's only 10:30, lover. Mind you, I might have to leave now to make it for lunch!" Bryony was nearing the end of her third trimester and it really showed now since she made no effort to hide it."

At lunch Sarah couldn't help but notice that she was the only one to drink two pints of the Hoyne on tap they always drank. Of course, Bryony didn't drink. Jo only had a couple of sips. When the bill arrived Jo grabbed it out of their usual waiters' hand. "This treat is on me", she announced, "to mark the end of Sarah's ordeal with that scum and...well,... I'm pregnant!" Jo had a grin wider than her face because she had successfully hidden it from the others. They were going to achieve their goal of what they saw as the perfect family.

Bryony struggled out of her seat and embraced Jo, showering her in kisses and tears of happiness. As her enthusiasm slowed slightly Sarah joined in making it a three person hug that attracted the attention of all the Fernwood's patrons. Sarah shouted, "She's pregnant too!". Spontaneous applause swept across the bar.

-19-

Walking around UVIC in the early spring was always a delight. So many different species of plants were shooting. Early rhodos were even flowering to match the prolific output of the daffodils and crocuses. For Sarah walking around the campus was a time to get lost in her thoughts, as she enjoyed the academic atmosphere where she had always felt so comfortable. Her inner voice had been after her for about a month since she had gone up Island. It was nagging her about what she was going to do with her life. Before the quake she had felt that she would go back to UVIC to become a teacher. With all the inheritance changes to her life, and Bryony expecting soon, Sarah's life decisions had been pushed to the back of her mind.

The vibration in her back pocket brought her back from her inner thoughts. It might be Bryony at the hospital, no, it was Sam. While exchanging greetings Sarah could tell something was wrong because Sam's voice didn't sound right.

"Sarah, Pete passed last night. I thought you should know."

"Sam, I'm so sorry for your loss. I know how close you are to him. Were to him." Sarah felt tears running down her cheeks as she sat on a bench with her head down.

"Yeh. Probably for the best. He was really suffering this past month and went fast at the end. Neither his pancreas nor liver worked, so he couldn't digest or metabolize food. You saw how thin he was getting when you were up. He was skin and bones at the end."

"What can I do to help, Sam? I can be up there in three hours after I get home. I have Dad's sixty-eight Mustang on the road now."

"There is not a lot to do right at the moment. The celebration of life is in four days."

"Tell you what, I'll come up in two days and help get things ready for the celebration of life. Can I speak at it?"

"Of course you can, Sarah. I don't know if I'll be able to. The ashes will go into the river the next day as he wished. His spirit will be carried by the salmon."

"I'll stay for that as well. Thanks for including me, Sam. I know this is a hard time for you. Know that my heart is with you."

"Thanks, Sarah. You can stay here when you come up."

Sarah continued walking around the grounds of the campus. Her thoughts now deflected to Pete, Sam and their family. She would figure out what to do about her future later. She somehow doubted if teaching was the correct choice. Having all this money had confused and complicated her decision making.

-20-

The celebration of life was probably typical in that a long-time family friend took on the master of ceremonies role, there was a song sung by two granddaughters, and the MC's wife and the other speakers had many funny and moving stories. Pete was well known and loved in the community, so the room was over-crowded and some people stood outside the entrance doors. Sarah hadn't been to many funerals but she was very moved when his grandson played Amazing Grace on the bagpipes. There were occasional teary moments before, but the pipes had moisture leaking from most of the eyes in the room. When Amazing Grace finished the family was piped out of the hall into the smaller hall next door where the food was served.

Sam was right, he couldn't speak about his dad at the ceremony. Instead he tried to speak to every person who had filled the main hall. Sarah joined some other women of the family, taking trays of food around to the assembled guests. She received many comments on her speech about Pete. It seemed that many people knew who she was, or had heard about her, the kayak trip, the shipwreck rescue, and they were glad to meet her. A few times her and Sam were asked to pose for pictures with other friends or family.

Back at the house, after cleaning up the hall, family and friends continuously dropped in for a drink and a chat. Sarah was kept so busy that she had no time to feel out of place or to notice the missed calls on her phone. In a lull in the action she checked the messages to find that Jo had been texting and phoning to tell her that Bryony had delivered a healthy baby girl. Mom and baby were both well. Sarah already knew the kid would be called Aurora Josephine. She was so excited for them, but had no one here to share that emotion with. She couldn't wait to get back to Victoria after the release of the ashes tomorrow. Eventually she did tell Sam about the baby. Poor guy, she had to tell somebody.

At 10:00 the next morning, only the closest family met at the Nymph Falls parking lot. Pete's sons carried the urn behind the grandson who piped all through the forest down to the falls. Sam apologized for not speaking the day before, and he managed not to get too choked up, explaining how important his dad had been to him in building houses and barns and all the adventures they had had together. The ashes were spread in the river as the pipes played Flowers of the Forest which echoed amongst the trees of the forest in the park.

Sam and Sarah walked together back up the trails to the car parking area. "Sam, thank you so much for letting me be a part of all this for the past few days."

"It's me who should be thanking you for all you've contributed to it."

"I really meant what I said yesterday about how important you and Pete have become in my life. You guys helped me figure huge chunks of my life out. And gain a massive amount of self-confidence."

"You still thinking about teaching?"

"This inheritance has put my ideas on pause a bit, so I've not applied for anything yet. Sam, I've been thinking, in honour of your Dad, we should complete the kayak trip around the Island. Start from Tofino and go south to Victoria and then back up the Salish Sea to Comox. What do you think?"

"I was thinking the same thing! I didn't know if you had the kind of time available that I do to complete the journey."

"You were considering it as well, so let's do it! When can you start?"

"Yeh, I just didn't know if you had the time and then who would I go with? I could leave soon. What do you think about May the first?"

"Sam, that sounds great. May the first. Let's shake on it."

Shaking on it, Sam couldn't miss the twinkle in Sarah's bright blue eyes. The plan was hatched out of a short conversation. They both knew continuing the trip was the right thing to do for Pete. They also knew it was something they both needed to do, so their lives wouldn't have any unfinished business.

-21-

Sarah enjoyed the drive back to Victoria in the sixty-eight Mustang. This one was a T5 that been put together in Mannheim, Germany, by an American forces member. The car had a specially geared rear end made for the German Autobahn, so what the car lacked in instant acceleration it made up for in top end speed. As a result Sarah had two delays coming down Island. First, was the inevitable Duncan crawl. Why had the highway not bypassed this city? The second delay was a speed trap near the start of the Malahat. Sarah lucked out however, because the policeman who should have ticketed her was more interested in the car initially, and then in her. She used some of the Bryony charm and got off with a warning. Sarah drove right at the speed limit the last forty kilometers to Victoria so as to not get stopped again.

She parked the Mustang in the garage and then walked straight over to Bryony and Jo's place. Sarah walked through the front door without knocking, running toward the bedroom, when she was intercepted by Jo coming out of the bedroom. "Ssshhh!", she whispered with her index finger up to her lips. "They have both just now fallen asleep. We need to let them sleep." Sarah hugged her regardless, and as she was offering congratulations Jo lead her back to the stools in the kitchen. "Coffee?"

"Yes please. How are you guys doing?" Sarah still had an abundance of excitement in her voice.

An obviously sleep-deprived Jo replied, "We are both over the moon but too tired to describe it. We are still running on adrenalin I guess." Jo passed a mug across to Sarah, "Here is your coffee, just the way you like it."

"I am so sorry I missed the birth. Give me the whole story, don't leave out a single detail."

"First, how was your trip? How was the funeral?"

They shared experiences back and forth for two hours, when they heard the ensuite toilet flush and the master bedroom door open to let Bryony out into the hall. Sarah was up in a flash and met her part way down the hall before she even made it to the kitchen. More hugs followed until Bryony detached herself from Sarah so she could receive the offered coffee from Jo.

"Well Mama, how is motherhood?"

"Thanks for the coffee, Jo. Isn't she the best caregiver ever? What was your ques…oh yes, love, I remember. Motherhood is like no experience I have ever had. But I've also never been this knackered in my life."

Jo added, "B. is a natural mom. I doubt I can be as good, eh. She is so good with little Aurora. Mind you the little one latched on straight away."

"Which is a good thing, lover, because I am making too much milk."

"Sarah, you should see her. Sometimes she is squirting milk all over the poor kids face!"

"It's a bit embarrassing, love. I had to look it up to see if I'm a weirdo. Guess what? It's actually not uncommon. And I can feel the pressure go down in my breasts. Apparently some women get so full their breasts hurt. Mine feel heavy, but no pain really. So far at least."

Bryony and Jo were so happy that Sarah could feel the positive vibe coming off of them. Suddenly the baby monitor squawked. Jo was up in a flash, returning with a slightly crying baby. She changed little Aurora right on the table to get her ready for a feeding from her mom. Afterward the little one was passed to Sarah to hold and rock back to sleep in the rocking chair. Sarah enjoyed the warmth and smell of Aurora while realizing, that this was great for Bryony and Jo, but that she was nowhere near ready for this for herself.

Jo woke Sarah up taking the baby out of her arms to put in her crib. "You fell asleep putting her to sleep! Too funny."

Before Sarah headed home she told them about her plans to finish kayaking around Vancouver Island with Sam to complete the trip they had started. Bryony and Jo encouraged her to do the trip while she still could, explaining how they could no longer do things like this. They had other responsibilities now. A different stage of life Sarah knew they would enjoy as much as the last stage. That was simply the kind of positive people they were.

-22-

The logistics of putting a trip together are always interesting. In the end, Sarah had Jo drive her up to Qualicum Beach with her kayak strapped on top of the BMW. They met Sam at the pullout on Highway Four near the Inland Highway. Sam had coffees and Danishes waiting for them. This gave Sarah a chance to properly introduce Sam to Jo. In no time they were chatting like they were old friends. Through what Sarah had told them they actually already did know a lot about each other. After thirty minutes of chatting it was time to go. It only took about ten minutes to transfer all the gear and the kayak to Sam's truck. Sarah wouldn't let Jo lift anything due to her pregnancy, and before they left warned her about getting a speeding ticket in the two hour drive back to Victoria. Sam and Sarah had three hours of driving ahead of them to get to Tofino.

Highway Four was only partially reopened due to bridges being out and rock slides at Kennedy Lake. All the delays made the trip take five hours. They arrived at Tofino tired, thirsty, and hungry, with too little of the day left to get far after loading their kayaks. Sam stashed the truck at the elementary school, where a friend would pick it up tomorrow to drive it back to the Comox Valley.

The significant tsunami damage of Tofino hadn't really changed much since Sam last saw it. Sarah thought Tofino was destroyed even worse than anywhere else she had seen. Damaged areas had all been cleaned up, but only the Government dock was being rebuilt at the moment. The line of sand deposited by the wave was still visible most places, even though much of the sand had been removed in the town. Only a couple of stores and no restaurants were open for business. Truth was that there were not many people around and no tourists to support businesses. What had always been a busy thriving port was now more like a ghost town. Another place that would take years to recover.

As they paddled out of the harbour, Sarah could feel the sadness of being in Tofino start to leave her body every time the blade of her paddle entered the water. She also felt a calm descend over her from being on the water and having finished all the prep work of the start of this leg of the trip. Or was it just the calm confidence of Sam projecting onto her? They had decided to try to camp at the south end of what was left of Vargas Island. What had been called Medallion Beach, a beautiful sandy beach few people used to ever go to due to the close proximity to Tofino.

As they skirted around where Stubbs Island had been, they had a clear view of the east side of Wickaninnish Island and further on to Vargas Island. The rocky parts were all that remained. All the vegetation was gone or lying flat. The tidal currents hadn't had enough time to reform the sandy beaches. Sam had been here many times but felt that without the trees and beaches, the whole area looked strangely different. The kelp beds hadn't regrown yet, making it weird to paddle without gliding through them. Only the numerous birds they encountered were reminiscent of how this place formerly felt and looked. Even their navigational charts were different now. Sam knew where Medallion Beach should be and guided them there.

"Well, Sarah, this used to be a sandy beach to camp on. Even had a toilet." Sam had rafted up beside Sarah as they scanned the rocky shore in front of them.

"There is a bit of sand reforming. Up there by all the logs," Sarah pointed out towards where she had observed the little bit of sand.

"The currents are really strong here. I still think it will be a long time before this is a sandy beach again."

"Sam, where should we try to stay tonight?"

"Good question. Everything is so different now. Everywhere we go on the outside of the Island we'll have to find new places to camp. We won't have this problem when we get to the Salish Sea, on the inside of the Island where the tsunami didn't have its way with the coast." The current and breeze had turned them so that now they could look at the remains of Lennard Lighthouse, which had been behind them. The politicians had promised to rebuild it and other important lighthouses, but so far nothing had been done. Sam suggested they paddle over to it and spend the night there. The chance they took was that if there was no spot to camp they would pretty much be stuck there for the night.

They found a little landing spot on the lee side of the island. With fiberglass kayaks they had to try to not land on rocky shores. The pebbles and rubble at this spot worked out perfectly. Sarah wondered if they would always be so fortunate. After getting the two kayaks up high enough, it was time to explore to see if they could find a camping spot. Sarah suggested they search together rather than splitting up.

Once off the beach they were confronted with a massive tangle of trees, driftwood and rubble from the lighthouse buildings. It didn't appear that anyone had been here to begin the rebuilding. Walking along the shore side of the jumble pile they found a better landing site and a trail that had been cut with chainsaws leading into the middle of the island. Sarah followed the trail a short distance and found a small clearing that had been made using the chainsaws. It was a perfect campsite.

She turned around to tell Sam they could camp here, but he wasn't there. Retreating the way she had come, she found Sam sitting on a log looking back towards Tofino. He looked deep in thought and pale.

"Sam, someone made a great campsite up there. With a years supply of firewood. You ok?"

He pulled himself out of his funk and turned towards her, "Right. Good. Let's move the kayaks and set up camp."

"You don't look so good."

"Not feeling that great. Let's get that pasta in us and I'll be a lot better."

As Sarah made her seafood linguini, Sam set up his tent and made a fire. There was only room for one tent here, so they decided to use his three-man MEC tent. Sarah hoped the snoring wouldn't be too bad and that in the future they would find places for two tents.

-23-

Sarah woke at first light feeling surprisingly refreshed, having slept right through the night. Glancing at Sam she could see that he was still sound asleep and breathing quietly. She didn't think he'd snored at all. Her inner voice congratulated her on having slept with a man. Sarah hadn't even thought about that since her attack. She was with a man, shouldn't she feel vulnerable? Was it weird that memories of that horrible night hadn't come flooding back to her? Did this mean she was all over what had happened to her? Was she whole again? Would she ever be whole again? Sam was like her dad, so in her deepest brain she must have felt safe. She would have to tell Sam about that horrific night. When it seemed right.

After telling her inner voice to shut up, she got out of the tent, got dressed and started heating some water on the stove, before going for her morning pee. When she came back to the stove she could hear a gentle snore coming from inside the tent. Sam had almost always been up before her previously. He looked very pale last night. Was he alright? She'd have to watch him carefully. She did notice that he'd gained a lot of weight from when they had been separated by the tsunami. They needed to talk more about that as well. And she'd never fully disclosed about her inheritance either.

Sarah had finished her porridge and was on her second cup of tea before the tent started rustling and shaking with grunts and grumbles. The fly flew open and a disheveled Sam made his way into the day. "Morning, Sarah." He was past her on his way to the beach before she could reply with words he would hear. It did make her smile, however, that nature was urgently calling for Sam.

As Sam came back up the trail Sarah met him with a cup of tea and chided him with, "Good afternoon, Sam."

"Thanks for the tea. It's only just gone eight!" Sitting on a stump he said, "Wow, that was some sleep. Did I keep you up with chainsaw noises?"

"No. In fact I slept right through to sunrise. When I woke up you were in the same position you went to sleep in. How do you feel this morning?"

"Yeh, I was feeling a bit rough last evening. Don't know what that was. Better today, I think. Sorry about that. It'll never happen again."

"Don't worry. If you are worried about doing this we can go back to Tofino. It gets harder to go back home as we head south."

"No, I'll be fine. Let's get on the water."

For their first full day of this leg they couldn't have had better conditions, so they paddled easily straight to Cox Point and the start of the Pacific Rim National Park. Or what was left of it. In many places the rocky shoreline seemed the same as always, each wave kicking up a flume of white surf. It was beyond the rock cliffs that things were different, but Sarah and Sam often couldn't see that sitting at water level in their kayaks, gently going up and down with the incoming swells. One thing that was the same as always was the little murres that would come up near the kayaks, realize something was there, and dive out of sight in what seemed like a panic. The murres always brought a smile to Sarah's face.

They ate lunch in their kayaks, drifting along outside the waves of Long Beach. They had heard that the tsunami had changed the profile of the famous surfing beach. The many people trying to surf didn't appear to care providing good entertainment to the kayakers. Sarah could never stand the cold north Pacific for as long as these dedicated surfers managed to do. Even with wetsuits on it was a mystery to her how they did it for hours at a time, day after day. With completely full bladders, they finally went to shore where Sandhill Creek entered the Pacific, providing a narrow promontory that allowed them to land without much of a surf landing. Sam was bursting and ran down the beach to empty his bladder. Sarah simply squatted under her skirt where she had landed. For once it was an advantage to be a woman.

Just past Quistis Point, while starting to cross Florencia Bay, they spotted two whale blows not far out from where they were. All that was visible was two large backs with small dorsal fins, one bigger than the other.

"Moving rocks," announced Sam without the enthusiasm he had for all the other cetaceans.

"Sam! Gray Whales might not put on as much a display as some others, but that mom and calf have come from Baja California and will go all the way to the Bearing Sea for the summer."

"You are right, Sarah. They are amazing in that their annual migration is possibly the longest by any mammal. Some of the locals call them moving rocks, because often that's all you get to see."

If it had been orcas or humpbacks they probably would have tried to see more of the whales. Instead they continued paddling south taking advantage of the calm conditions. The sea state was only about a meter with very little wind. Before long they could see Amphitrite Point which gave them a target for the day that was further south than they could have hoped for. Sarah kept periodically checking on Sam, worrying about his little bout the day before. Truth to be told though, the older man was out-paddling her. They spent the night in a sheltered bay at the end of the Ucluelet Peninsula where there was plenty of room for two tents and they even had a wee bit of sand.

-24-

Crossing the open water of Barkley Sound didn't seem like a good idea especially with a westerly of 10-20 knots predicted. Two to three meter swells added to Sarah and Sam making the choice to paddle into the Broken Islands group of islands that would provide shelter from winds and waves as they headed south. Both Sarah and Sam were not big fans of open water crossings, so the day started with a good pace that they would keep up until they reached more sheltered waters. It wasn't just feeling less safe while crossing. It was also far less interesting out there with less to see, so they just got on with reaching the other side.

They encountered two more pairs of migrating gray whales while crossing Loudoun Channel. Like yesterday they didn't stop much to watch the moving rocks. Nor did they talk much, leaving Sarah wondering when she would tell Sam about her ordeal and the full details of her inheritance. Maybe she'd just let the latter come out when they got to Victoria. The campfire some night might be the best time for the former. The first couple of campfires had not been like when Pete was with them. Sam obviously missed his old man. Perhaps she could get him talking about that.

By mid-morning they had reached the lea side of Benson Island. There was a campsite there, now gone, but it still provided a short rest stop. Paddling was easier on the calmer water but they still didn't talk much other than about what they saw or where they were headed next. Sarah wondered if she misremembered what their trip had been like going around the north Island. Or was it Pete that triggered the conversations she recalled? When they agreed to complete this circumpaddle of the Island, Sam made it clear that much of his motivation was to complete the journey for his dad. Sarah was onboard for that, but wanted to finish the trip to complete her healing and search for her future direction. So far she felt it wasn't working as expected. Her inner voice screamed that she needed to give it more time. Sometimes, her inner critic was correct, and she knew it.

A short open crossing found them behind Cooper Island providing very sheltered paddling to Bowke and Austin Islands with the large Effingham Island to their east. Effingham had elevations high enough to have survived the tsunami untouched. The tall trees there were filled with the white heads and tails of mature bald eagles like ornaments on Christmas trees. With no nesting or perching trees on the smaller islands the eagles appeared to have declared territorial truces so they could still have a branch to stand on while majestically watching over their world like the royalty they are.

Before the tsunami, Austin Island had had a decent sized campsite on it. When Sarah and Sam landed on it they found few clues to suggest humans had ever been here. At one time they were aware the Nuu-chah-nulth people had lived on these islands or at least had fish camps on them. There were no signs people had been here since the quake. Sarah felt like stretching her legs, so they walked over much of the south and eastern parts of the island. It was interesting to see how vegetation was returning to reclaim the island. Small knots of grasses and even small shrubs like evergreen huckleberries were starting to take hold in less than a year. They also found a few small conifer trees starting their lives out on the rocky island. One had to wonder how their seeds had even got there.

Sarah pointed out a small clump of seedlings to Sam saying, "The succession of new life to a place like this is incredible. Nature at work despite all we and other things throw at it. After us humans are gone it won't take long to recover. Mother Nature again showing us who is really in charge."

"No doubt," he replied. "I have always marveled at how fast life starts to come back when it is removed. Like the areas that were wiped out by Mount St. Helens in 1980. I knew an English biologist who took students to Iceland to study succession after volcanic activity. He said that in one place they studied somehow a species of fish were in a natural pool only five years after the lava and debris flow. They could only speculate how they got there and they knew they were not there the summer before."

"It is incredible. That park at St. Helens after thirty years had most of the original species return. Even the beavers were back!"

"I heard about that. 'Something else' is what the old man would say."

"Still missing him a lot, Sam?"

"Suppose I always will. Being here, doing this, with you, I don't know…it's like he should be here. I am sure glad you are here. And we are completing what we started. In his memory."

Sarah broke the long silence that followed, "Let's stay here tonight. The wind has come up this afternoon as usual, so crossing Imperial Eagle Channel will be easier in the morning."

They set up camp near to where they had landed. After the tents were set up they found washed up planks which they turned into a nice kitchen spot out of the wind. After dinner they watched the sun go down as two sea otters floated past them laying on their backs, eating and cracking urchins on rocks held on their chests.

Sarah woke the next morning to the sounds of the weather reports on the radio. Sam was up early. Perhaps things were getting back to normal. Like it had been before. She wasn't the same, though, and she still hadn't told Sam about what had happened to her.

Sarah had barely gotten out of the tent before Sam had a cup of tea in her hands. Taking her first sip of the hot sweet liquid, she realized the sea fog had descended on them. Visibility was very limited so they wouldn't be in a hurry to get off the beach this morning. They could only hope it would burn off or blow away. As kayakers they didn't prefer the latter unless it was a gentle breeze. They didn't have far to go today anyway. She decided it was a good day to enjoy the pancakes Sam was making and perhaps a second cup of tea, a rare treat on a kayak trip.

Effingham Island had an interesting sea arch to look at, but by the time they launched that larger island was still hanging onto the fog while they had a clear route over to the Deer Group of Islands about two hours away. Sam said there was another sea arch for them to see at King Edward Island.

They crossed Imperial Eagle Channel easily as the afternoon winds were not up yet, and they paddled into the lea side of King Edward Island for a rest and lunch. Seeing the winds coming up the decision to cross Trevor Channel over to Bamfield was easily reached, even though they had lots of time and the crossing was only an hour. There would be no sea arches today. Nearing the narrow entrance to Bamfield Inlet they noticed two whale blows close to the shore. As they paddled towards the inlet it appeared they would not encounter the two humpback whales for they could judge by the frequency of their blows as they headed west towards the open Pacific. Nevertheless, Sam had them stop before the mouth of the inlet outside of the route the whales had been taking.

"Sam, it's been a lot longer between blows this time. Wonder where they have gone? Should we go on now?"

"Let's wait a bit longer. Have you been watching all the activity in Bamfield? They are rebuilding docks and what have you like there is no tomorrow."

"I know, right. See all the people looking at the whales up where the marine station was?", Sarah asked it as a question.

Sam never got a chance to answer because about fifty feet off their bows a humpback lunged upwards out of the water.

It's rorquals filled with water stretching the skin massively. Fish and water came out of it's mouth where gulls appeared from nowhere to get a meal as the whale sank back into the water. The second whale lunged upwards beside it and the gulls got another feed.

"Holy shit! They could have been right under us! Then what?"

"Sarah, you ok? That was better than what we saw before the tsunami. In the awesome presence of greatness, eh."

"I know this is the second time we've seen this, but I held my breathe the whole time. Look, here comes a boat."

Sure enough a zodiac was racing towards them stopping right in front of them. "We thought you two were gonners. That's what it looked like from back there," shouted the man on the bow.

Sarah said, "So did I, but we're fine. It was like fifty feet in front of us. You didn't need to check on us. Thanks though."

"Everyone watching from the harbour was yelling at us to get out here, since we were already in the zodiac. Coming in to Bamfield?"

"Is it ok if we do? I was here right after the 'quake. Left on the Tully."

"I remember it being here," said the older man in the stern. "Come on in. Not much here now, but we are starting to rebuild."

Sam said, "From here it looks like you are ahead of Tofino. They have no docks yet."

After checking out the harbour Sam and Sarah decided to not even land. It just looked too devastated. They paddled out of the harbour heading west along the Mills Peninsula to the easy landing at Brady's Beach. Here they could camp and prepare for the fully exposed paddling ahead, as they headed down the Pacific Rim National Park where the West Coast Trail was.

-25-

Sarah woke at first light to find Sam already up, tea made and water boiled for the porridge. Conditions were really calm, so they multi-tasked and were off the beach in an hour. It had been suggested to them that they shouldn't try to round Cape Beale because of all the boomers and rocks, especially at lower tides. There was a 'shortcut' portage available at low tides at the small cove used to supply the lighthouse that Sarah and Sam were considering. The thought against walking across the little isthmus was that portages take a lot of time and energy. In the back of Sarah's mind was always to get as far as possible before the afternoon winds came up.

At the lighthouse they checked the lighthouse reports again on the radio. With an incoming tide and low sea state, conditions were nearly perfect for going outside. They had to watch very carefully for boomers, only glancing quickly at the old lighthouse site. Two hours after breaking camp they went to shore at the western end of the beautiful two kilometer long Keeha Bay.

Sarah went right as usual to relieve herself. Returning to the kayaks she noticed Sam walking away from the beach to what looked like a series of caves. She caught up to Sam just as he was entering the nearest cave. It had been carved into the rock by millennia of waves whittling away at weaknesses in the rock. The opening was about twenty feet across and probably fifteen feet high, narrowing quickly towards the back, which was filled with driftwood and debris.

"Sam, do you smell that?"

"For sure. Something's dead in here. Want to look?"

"I'm alright. You go ahead. I'll check out the next cave. I didn't know these caves were here."

At the mouth of the next cave Sarah could smell that same dank nose offending stink. She was about to turn around when her eye, adjusting to the lack of light, caught sight of a large white object sticking out of the driftwood at the back of the cave. She pulled her shirt up and held it covering her nose and mouth and slowly walked into the cave until she realized she was looking at a large whale bone. Perhaps a humerus from a humpback whale she was thinking, when something touched her left elbow giving her a shock.

"Sam! You scared the hell out of me."

"Sorry. There was nothing this interesting in the other cave."

Sarah had let go of her shirt exposing her nose to the smell again. "Let's get out of here, I can't breathe!".

Sarah was pretty sure she held her breath until she was well clear of the cave. Gulping clean air didn't seem to make that horrible smell go away. Back at the kayaks to drink some water, Sarah insisted they paddle on. Sam never said but she was pretty sure he wanted to explore the caves more.

Sarah felt her lungs finally clear, with the help of the fresh sea air, after paddling forty-five minutes across Keeha Bay. The much wider and deeper Pachena Bay stood open in front of them. Since they still had two hours until noon, and no signs of wind yet, they paddled at a strong steady pace reaching Mabena Beach as the afternoon winds made their predictable appearance. After lunch and a snooze Sam suggested they stay there for the night, get rested and make a really early start tomorrow which would be smart as the radio informed them conditions would be the same as the last few days.

After dinner Sam told Sarah about hiking the West Coast Trail and that where they were camped was near the northern end of the trail. He took her up a steep trail through and around considerable tsunami debris until they were above it to discover the now abandoned West Coast Trail. They walked south to a couple of different vantage points to view the spectacular vistas of the west coast. As before, she was in awe of how wild it all was. And that they were going to paddle it!

The next morning they were up at 5:00, which Sam called, "Zero dark thirty" for some reason. A thick sea fog greeted them, but they decided to paddle regardless, because the sea was relatively calm, and the swells were as small as they ever got around there. One had to go when the going was good. Besides, the fog was supposed to be gone soon. She thought Sam must be getting into this trip now because he was singing a song like he had on the pre-quake parts of the adventure. It was "'Feeling Alright'" by Traffic. Sarah realized she hadn't heard Sam singing since they left Tofino.

This was the first time. She thought it was all part of the healing involved in Pete's passing.

Rounding Pachena Point in the fog, paddling just outside the surf wasn't ideal for seeing where you were. The fog had a way of disorientating the brain. Sarah was convinced it was worse for her than Sam who had optic nerve damage vision problems working against him as well as the fog. He claimed he was always 'in the fog'. She thought he was very well adapted to living in a world of poor vision. Sarah knew there would be no boat traffic this close to land making it safe to be where they were. They followed the shoreline to the east for a bit and went to shore at Michigan Creek when the sun finally started to break through.

The coastline was different in this part of Vancouver Island. For as far as Sarah could see the shoreline was practically straight without any prominent headlands or big bays. In many places there was a wide shelf right at the high tide line often made up of dark coloured, very hard, basalt rock. Sometimes the shelf was half a kilometer wide with periodic deep tidal surges that usually went all the way up to the base of the cliffs lining the beaches. It reminded her of the shelves at Barcester Bay, only here there was usually high cliffs at the edge of sea and land.

The afternoon winds came later in the day, so they kept paddling after noon, only stopping when they reached Tsusiat Falls. A spectacular waterfall that fell over the cliffs directly onto the intertidal area. From the sea it appeared to fall directly into the Pacific. The falls were fed by a lake of the same name and in the later spring still had plenty of water flowing over them. They landed on a shingle beach just below the falls where there had been a popular camp-site for the West Coast Trail. With the trail closed Sarah and Sam had the beach to themselves. They quickly set up camp and decided to go explore around the falls. Sarah hadn't noticed but Sam grabbed a towel and bar of soap before he left camp, while she was still finishing putting her tent together.

When Sarah got to the falls Sam was standing under the far side of them clad only in his underwear having a shower. "How's the water?", she enquired.

"A wee bit nippy, but really refreshing", came the reply. "I hope I am not offending you in my skivvies."

Sarah was deciding whether to shower as well as she watched Sam lather himself up with his soap. In this climate it would take forever for her underwear and hair to dry. Once things got wet on the coast, they never seemed to get dry again. What the hell, she thought she might never do something like this again so she stripped everything off and moved into the waterfall about as far as possible from Sam who was lathering up his hair and had his eyes closed. Without his glasses on she knew he couldn't see her very well. The waterfall was quite wide so if she went on the other side of it she didn't think he'd be offended, and she felt safe that he wouldn't take it the wrong way. Her inner voice claimed Sam wouldn't even notice. The cold water sure felt good flowing over her body. She liked the way her skin tingled. She had taken her ample hair out of its usual bun and she loved how the pounding water flattened it against her back. As she looked out to sea two gray whales were feeding right in front of them.

When Sam opened his eyes he glanced at her but only spoke to point out the two whales and offer her the soap. Showering like this seemed so natural. When she had completely washed, Sam insisted she use the towel first and he stayed under the falls actually looking the other way as she dried and dressed, glad to not have wet clothes to deal with.

"Sam, thanks for the towel. I'll leave it on this log for when you come out." Sarah walked back to camp feeling totally refreshed, listening to her inner critic going on about her teasing this old man over forty years her senior and telling her she shouldn't have done it. But did it ever feel good. And how many people can say they had a shower under a waterfall on a beach on the Pacific Ocean with two whales feeding a hundred meters in front of you? Her inner critic really bothered her sometimes.

After dinner Sarah settled beside a large log to support her back. She wiggled back and forth to make a depression in the shingle for her seat. Once settled she focused her attention on the ocean in front of her, watching the birds go about their business.

Sam had finished the dishes and came over to join her hanging his still wet underwear on a driftwood root. "You did the right thing at the falls, these shorts will never dry out here."

"Sam, I'm sorry about that. I probably shouldn't have showered like that."

"No apology needed. If I was your age and looked as gorgeous as you, I would have done the same thing. Sarah you are only young once. Take advantage of it I say because you'll get old and crinkly like me before you know it. Carpe diem, life is here to enjoy."

"Thanks for saying that." Sarah thought there might never be a better time than now to tell Sam her two secrets. "Sam, I have something to tell you that I've been holding back. Looking for an opportunity. Can I bare my sole to you?"

"Absolutely. You don't have to ask, you know."

"It's just that when I got back to Victoria I lived on my parents' property in a tent because the house was ruined by the quake and tsunami. One night three assholes pulled me out of the tent. Two held my arms and legs while the ringleader set out to … well, rape me." She burst into tears despite thinking she was past that stage of grief. But this was Sam. Someone special.

"Oh Sarah. You poor kid." Sam moved closer and gave her a big hug until she recovered her composure.

"Sorry, I wasn't going to lose it in telling you. Wrong. Anyways, I got my right hand free and grabbed his scrotum just as he entered me. I raked my nails along him and managed to get a leg free to knee him in the privates as well. He ended up curled up in pain on the grass. My screams brought help but his buddies took their boots to me before they made their escape."

"Jesus. The sons of bitches! Did they get away with it?"

"No. I reported it and they caught all three of them. After Pete's funeral I went back to Vic for the trial of the ringleader. It didn't happen because he committed suicide the morning of the trial. I think he had six more trials after mine."

"Wow. I hate it when bad things happen to good people. How are you dealing with all of this?"

"I thought I was doing well. My tears now suggest otherwise."

"No, Sarah, they don't. You are grieving as much as I am, I mean we are, about losing Pete. It all takes time and will never totally go away. What matters now is what you do with it to not let those ignorant buggers negatively affect your life. They don't have the right to impact your future."

"Thanks, Sam. And, of course, I know all of this. I've been told it all before. It's complicated though. To get your confidence and self-esteem back is not as easy as it seems. So I haven't told you that while getting my inheritance I met two incredible women who have helped me tremendously. I now live near them and spend a lot of time with them. Jo, who you met, is one of them. And Sam, I also haven't told you, or anyone for that matter, about how wealthy I am now. My parents left me four houses and investments worth millions. That Mustang you have seen is only one of several antique cars my dad left behind."

"I had no idea of any of this Sarah. Don't let any of it change who you are. You are perfect the way you are!"

"Awe, Sam. How does it feel to be president of my fan club?"

"It feels good, especially sitting here enjoying this scenery, and I know I am not the only member of the club!"

"So yeh, I think I'm doing well about all this. So now I have to decide what to do with my life with all these recent changes. That'll be my mission on the rest of this kayak trip."

"Right you are then. It's good to know what our mission is on this trip. Honour Pete and sort out what you are going to do with your life. Should be easy! Ha ha." Sam knew how to get her laughing. "You know I am here to help any way I can. You've got this, Sarah."

"And here comes the evening entertainment." Sam pointed just to the south of them as a gray whale mom and her calf were feeding. "The water must be shallow there because they seem to be at the surface a lot."

Sarah made no reply. She hugged her knees in the relief of having told Sam her secrets. She hated it when she put things off like she had about explaining the assault to Sam. When she delayed things such as that the subject haunted her. Always in the back of her mind, jumping to the front of mind far too often. Now it was out and she didn't have to carry it around with her anymore. It also provided a warm feeling knowing she would have Sam's ear and support whenever needed. Seeing how the calf stayed so close to her mom made her think that at this moment she was like that with Sam. She had never felt that way with her own father. She released her knees and snuggled into the side of the older man laying her head on his shoulder. How was it that she could get more support and comfort from Sam than she ever had from her own father?

That last thought gave her restless legs so she got up and followed the whales towards the sunset to the west until she felt settled. By the time she got back to camp it was getting dark. Sam wished her goodnight giving her a big hug. Sarah went to sleep wondering when the last time her father had given her a hug goodnight.

-26-

Sarah woke to the sounds of pots rattling in their kitchen area. She got up quickly to find that Sam wasn't up yet. All their pots and plates were on the ground. As she picked them up she saw the evidence of how they got there. Wolf prints were all over the area including around their tents. Looking up and down the beach provided no sight of the opportunistic thieves. Sam and her were always very careful about not leaving anything out for the various camp robbers that included crows, ravens, gulls, mice, rats, racoons, martins, wolves and even bears. You couldn't even have anything in your tent. Not even toothpaste.

Sarah got water from the falls and made the tea. Sam was still not up. The lure of the falls and the wonderful feeling of yesterday took Sarah back to the falls with a bar of soap and a towel. It would feel great to wash her sticky sleep skin. She recalled the comment from yesterday about how many times in your life can you have a shower under a waterfall facing the open Pacific Ocean? The water was cool but not much different from yesterday. It invigorated all of her skin making her feel totally alive. After yesterday she realized she hadn't felt this whole since the assault. Her nipples certainly hadn't, standing at full attention same as yesterday. When she touched them she realized all of her skin was alive and tingling. Feeling this alive might get her past her feelings of anxiety, fear, and violation. Maybe she'd swim in the sea every morning the rest of their trip. Just a thought if it was going to make her feel this complete.

Drying off and dressing, Sarah was aware that this was the best she had been physically and mentally, maybe ever. And all it took to heal her was an old man, a kayak, and a waterfall! She knew the assault would be with her for the rest of her life, but this was the closest to being healed she'd been yet. She felt on top of the world in a magical place on the planet.

Back at the camp Sam was still snoring away the morning in his tent. Sarah listened to the forecasts and lighthouse reports which were still very favorable. She made a tea for Sam and woke him up. It felt good to deliver him a tea since it was usually the other way round.

Paddling conditions continued to be near ideal. Tomorrow they were expecting a low pressure system to come in bringing rain and winds from the southwest. Lucky for them Cape Flattery somewhat protected this part of the Island from the southwesterlies. They lunched at Clo-oose Bay and made it to the Carmanah Point Lighthouse mid-afternoon as the clouds started to come in off the Pacific. Not really knowing what tomorrow would bring, the decision to get to the Walbran Creek campsite for the night was easy to reach.

They set up camp and ate in light rain and winds, but the forecasts predicted a much heavier storm to hit them around midnight. Sam made a decent fire that they sat around under their umbrellas. Sarah thought that anybody seeing them would think they looked pretty funny. This camp wasn't very far from Port Renfrew and the start of the West Coast Trail, yet they still saw no other humans. And with the storm approaching, the birds and animals all seemed to melt into the forest. After all the conversation of the day before, the campfire talk was lively mostly centered on the protection of the Carmanah Valley. Sarah had heard all Sam's arguments before and didn't disagree with him about trying to keep all the remaining old growth forests for all the creatures dependent on them, and for our future generations. Much of the Island had been logged already and the industry no longer provided the number of jobs it once did. Most of the sawmills and virtually all the pulp mills were now closed. Cities like Port Alberni, Powell River and Nanaimo had had to reinvent themselves. Smaller towns like Port Alice and Gold River hadn't become ghost towns as some predicted, although their futures were far from secure.

With Sam droning on, Sarah was glad the noise of rain on her umbrella had increased. The wind was also coming up, so it was easy to convince Sam that it was bedtime.

Sarah slept like a baby that night. The pitter-patter of rain drops on her tent completely filling the edges of her consciousness. When early daylight filled her tent she could only roll over and slip in and out of sleep, telling her bladder to hold on until the rain stopped. Which it never did. Sam scratched on her fly to tell her that he'd put tea under it.

Poking her head out with the tea in hand she could see the gentle waves hitting the shingle beach. She felt like they were calling her to go for a swim. She took off her undies and sleeping shirt, told Sam to look away, and ran down the beach diving into a wave once she could no longer run in the water. The water was colder than it had been at Tsusiat Falls but she had all the same feelings she had experienced the last two days. She didn't spend more than five minutes swimming and now she knew this would be her new routine. However, skinny dipping would have to end soon when they got around people again. For now she would just take advantage of the opportunity, and feel good!

Two hours of paddling in steady rain had them at the entrance to Port Renfrew called Port San Juan. Sarah described what she had seen there when she was on the Tully. They decided to keep going to put to shore for lunch and relief at Sombrio Point. This beach was near the top of the Juan De Fuca Trail. It had been one of the hippy settlements in the 1970's, some of which still remained. While raining, the weather wasn't actually too bad yet. The swells hadn't grown beyond about two meters and the further south they got the more protected they were by Cape Flattery and the Olympic Peninsula and the mountains of Washington State. It made sense to keep going. Sarah felt reborn after Tsusiat Falls and her morning swim, so she felt extra-ordinarily energetic, while Sam seemed to be one of those paddlers who could go on forever. "No wonder", Sarah thought, "his arms were like tree trunks." She remembered the first time she had hugged Sam. She couldn't get her arms around his shoulders and chest he was so well built. He'd have no trouble continuing on.

Rounding San Simeon Point, Sarah peered at China Beach where the blue, red and, yellow tent tarps and flies convinced Sam they should go even further to the Jordan River Campsite another hour away. They got a few hours reprieve from the rain accompanied by a rise in the wind. Neither Sam nor Sarah were really bothered by the rain. This was a rain forest after all! After a long, wet slog, Sarah decided to pay for a campsite so they could have a shower and cook under a shelter. Sam wouldn't have done this, however, they were around people now, why not take advantage of the amenities?

Both Sam and Sarah weren't enjoying the drunken campers in the cook shed so they only stayed long enough to eat and clean up. Afterwards, they walked the beach watching the eagles and gray whales until rain started again, this time pushed in by strong winds leaving them wondering how the paddle would go tomorrow. They were now only two days of paddling from Victoria. Sarah wondered about calling Jo and Bryony to come and pick them up. She didn't suggest it to Sam knowing he needed to paddle the whole route.

Sarah and Sam left Jordan River before most of the campers were even awake. The rain and wind had blown themselves out over-night. The sea state was less than expected making progress as quick as ever, especially since the wind got channeled between Vancouver Island and the Olympic Peninsula turning it to push them eastward along the Juan De Fuca Strait. They rounded Point No Point before 10:00 and passed Sheringham Point lighthouse by 11:00. After lunch at a creek in Orveas Bay the winds rose to twenty knots. By staying as close to the shore as they could they still made good progress and decided to camp by themselves on the beach just before Beechey Head.

Being alone, Sam felt safe getting a small fire going after dinner ignoring how close they were to civilization. He built it in a hollow below a pile of driftwood. When they both settled in around the mesmerizing flames Sam said, "This is better. No riff-raff around us."

"Those campers bothered you didn't they?" Sarah was using her thumbnails to scratch her chipped nail polish off, thinking Bryony and Jo would do her nails when she got home. Surprised she hadn't broken any on the trip, she had found that the saltwater only seemed to help her nails and skin. She knew it wasn't that way for everyone.

"I'll admit it. They convince themselves they are going into the wilds. Then they pack all the amenities of home in their trailers or campers so they live just like they do at home. And then they spend all night drinking. They didn't even try to see the nature right near them."

"I know what you mean. In that whole campsite, do you think anyone else saw the eagles or whales we saw?"

"Doubt it. I call them cidiots."

"I know, Sam. At least they leave the city for the weekend."

"I guess. So the plan for tomorrow is to get to your place in Victoria?"

"Weather permitting."

-27-

The weather calmed down during the night. Following breakfast and Sarah's quick swim they followed the coast eastwards towards Victoria with a ten knot wind pushing them along. Sam had been watching the shore, "Sarah, I'm sure the tsunami didn't go as far up the shore here as what we saw before."

"For sure. We could really see it when we steamed in here on the Tully. By the time the wave got to this part of the Island it was smaller than it was at Tofino. Last time I was here the smoke from burning Victoria buildings was very obvious. When we round Race Rocks today we won't see anything like that."

At William Head, while taking a short break, Sarah decided to call Bryony and Jo. "B., it's Sarah."

"Sarah, love! We were just talking about you. Where are you? I'll put you on speaker, Jo is right here."

"Hi Jo. We're having a bathroom break near William Head."

"Hi Sarah. Jo here. Good to hear your voice! There's a prison there. Hope you're not in it!"

"No, we're not inmates. Yet."

Bryony said, "Sarah, you are basically in Victoria now. We must come and pick you up and dinner is here tonight."

Bryony didn't ask questions about things like this and she was almost impossible to say no to. "B. and Jo that is very generous of you to offer. Our idea was to paddle all the way around the Island! Sam is back from his walk, let me talk to him and I'll call back."

"O…K. If he is not up for it let me talk to him, love."

"Got it. Bye for now."

Sam sat on the log beside Sarah. "Who's that?", he asked nodding toward the phone.

"Bryony and Jo. My friends who I've told you about. They want to pick us up and make us dinner tonight."

"Hmmm. I don't know. You live near there, right?"

"Same street."

"So we could shower and get cleaned up. I've only got camping duds."

"I'll get you something to wear. It'll work out."

Back on the phone with Bryony, it was agreed that they would meet in a couple of hours at Whittys Lagoon Park, just before Metchosin. Bryony had a new Outback to carry their soon to be two babies, that could easily take the two kayaks.

When the call was finished Sam said, "I thought something like this might happen when we got here, after the bits you've told me about them."

"So you're really alright about not paddling past Victoria and Esquimalt Harbours?"

"I guess I'll survive." Actually, faced with the possibility, Sam was looking forward to getting cleaned up and eating non-camp food.

When they got to the Lagoon Park the white Suburu was already there with Jo leaning against it watching them paddle the last of Parry Bay. Bryony was finishing feeding little Aurora in the front seat as they landed. Hugs and introductions followed. Before any unloading of kayaks could be done, Sarah and Sam each had a cold local craft beer thrust into their hands.

After a long first pull on the beer Sam proclaimed, "Nectar of the gods!"

Sarah said, "I know, it never tastes better than after a trip. Or during it in our case."

Bryony and Jo could only watch them, "Man, do I wish I could join you but we are booze-free now. And I'm not drinking until Jo is finished breast-feeding."

"B., you don't have to do that. She's so good to me!"

Sarah felt a buzz from the beer after only a couple of sips. It certainly made the loading of the kayaks go quicker. Before she knew it they were heading back to Victoria with Sam and her with Aurora in the back seat. Jo was driving and Bryony was half turned backwards to face them while she grilled them with questions about their trip so far. The beer and car motion soon had Sarah and Sam feeling sleepy, providing progressively shorter responses until Bryony gave up letting them fall asleep.

Sarah was well aware she had slipped away to dreamland while trying not to. When the car stopped in her driveway she came to with a startled expression on her face. Sam groggily came back to reality at the same time. Sarah apologized for falling asleep, "So sorry, Bryony. Falling asleep mid-conversation. How rude."

"Don't even think about it, love. We use the car to put the little human to sleep as well."

They unloaded the gear and kayaks around the back of Sarah's house and agreed to meet for supper. Sarah gave Sam a quick tour insisting he hit the showers on the main floor. She offered him a fresh towel and some of her Dad's old clothes to wear, while they washed his kayaking clothes that really smelled of fire smoke inside the house.

Sarah showered in her ensuite. The hot water felt so cleansing, especially when she turned the hot tap up. Her tingling pink skin reminded her again of how whole she presently felt, so she switched to cold water only to see if it had the same effect as swimming in the sea. Close, but no cigar, she thought.

After drying herself she could hear Sam in the kitchen and pulled a summer dress on and went to see what he was up to. "Finding what you need?"

"Just making us some tea. Found everything we need except, do have any honey?"

"In the one below the mugs. I'll go dry my hair then and tea will be ready when I'm done."

After tea, Sarah showed Sam her dad's car collection on their way out of the house to go over to Bryony and Jo's for dinner. Sarah took two bottles of wine off the rack before leaving, giving Sam an idea of what the evening had in store for them.

At the front door, Sarah didn't knock or ring the bell, she simply opened the door and invited Sam in. He was greeted with the rich cumin curry smell of a madras curry dish followed by more hugs and kisses from Bryony and Jo. At the table Sam felt intimidated by the company he was keeping. These three women were what he would call 'head-turners'. They were like a power trio who could use their looks and presence to dominate any situation if they chose. Jo with her long blonde hair, red lips and nails might catch the eye first. Sam's eye then went to Bryony who reminded him of Catherine Zeta-Jones, except she had blue eyes. And Sarah fit right in with these two. He was old enough to be the father of all of them yet he somehow felt out of his league amongst them, despite Bryony and Jo doing everything possible to make him feel included. The power of beautiful women! Sam thought, if only they knew the power they had. He was soon to discover that Bryony and Jo did know, and they used it to their advantage.

Conversation that night was mostly on their kayak trip and on the recovery from the quake and tsunami. Aurora hardly interrupted at all. Just a quick feed and change and back to bed. Sarah saw Sam visibly relax as the night wore on and he felt more comfortable around her friends. At the end of the night both bottles of wine were empty and Sarah knew there was only two of them drinking. Walking home Sarah grabbed Sam's upper arm saying, "You sure were quiet at the start of the night."

Sam gave her a sideways glance, "Suppose I just needed some time to settle in with your buddies."

"At first I didn't think you liked them."

"Oh Sarah. Sorry. Truth is I don't think I've ever been around three more gorgeous women in my life. I was intimidated."

"Wow. I didn't know people felt like that."

"You underestimate yourself too much, Sarah. Too many women do. The cool thing about Jo and Bryony is that they don't. In fact I think they use it for their own benefit."

Sarah thought back to when she first met them, "You're right, Sam. They do. I've seen them do it. And they really do affect men. And get what they want. When you get to know them you'll see they are delightful."

"I can see that now. I'm just lucky to hang out with people like you three."

Sarah squeezed his huge arm against her side. She hadn't really thought of herself as on the same level as Bryony and Jo until Sam included her with them.

-28-

Sarah and Sam ended up spending six days in Victoria. Sarah seemed to have different things to do each day, including legal and landlord duties. She took him to her other properties like Dallas Road where they talked about what she was going to rebuild there. Sarah took Sam around the inner harbour to see the ruination, and though the clean-up was complete, rebuilding had not yet been started. The museum and parliament had both found temporary quarters inland. Plans to rebuild were tied up in controversy and red tape. The Empress was not going to be rebuilt so it appeared the local First Nations were going to take over the site, constructing administrative buildings and a museum on the land that at one time was a swamp across the bay from their village.

Bryony and Jo hosted Sarah and Sam each night for dinner, games, and conversation that went late into the evening. Twice Sam ended up asleep in the rocking chair, with little Aurora asleep on his chest. Sarah had a spa day getting all made up by Bryony and Jo while Sam looked after Aurora until she needed mom. As he got to know Bryony and Jo, he loosened up around them starting to joke with them like he did with Sarah. Each night the three women would dress up for dinner while Sam only had shorts and a t-shirt on so he started giving them a hard time about what they were wearing. On the last night Sarah insisted Sam wear a suit of her father's that she had rescued from Dallas Road. She even made him wear a tie. She wanted to see the reaction of Bryony and Jo.

They arrived at six o'clock precisely, but Sarah rang the doorbell this time and made them stand outside on the covered porch. Bryony opened the door and stood back with a shocked look on her face. "We finally got to you, love!" Then, "Jo you got to see what the cat dragged in. Tidy!"

Jo only said, "Impressive." She looked Sam up and down and then it was the usual hugs and kisses. Sam felt silly going along with Sarah's little joke, but it worked. Then he took notice of Bryony in a form fitting red dress and heels and Jo in a full length black dress. Sarah had a flowery short summer dress on with black heels. He realized they were probably more formally dressed than him.

That night they had pot roast with Yorkshire pudding made by Bryony. "This is what my mom made every Sunday to start the week right. I thought it would be good to start the next leg of your trip right."

Sarah replied, "Delicious, as usual. It has been wonderful having you two fattening us up each night. Thanks so much."

"This has been a wonderful week. Thanks so much you two. I wish you'd make more of an effort on the dressing up…", Sam teased.

Bryony cut him off, "Those are the first decent clothes you've worn all week."

Sarah stopped the laughing proposing a toast, "To good friends." Glasses clinked and they all said the toast together.

Sam said, "What are we discussing tonight?"

Bryony answered, "I've been thinking about this and I think we need an in depth discussion of the growth of right wing populace governments worldwide. How long will they last and what will end them?"

Silence greeted this as the others considered her suggested topic. Jo asked, "Does this include fundamentalist states like Iran and Afghanistan under the Taliban?"

"I suppose it does, love. I was thinking of the move in democracies like south of the border. Or like next door in Alberta. Sarah says she always enjoyed your talks around the campfire, Sam. What do you think?"

Sam was stroking his mustache as he considered what Bryony had introduced. "We did have good talks out there, eh Sarah? The ones around this table have been just as good. I think conservatism globally is in big trouble as they align themselves with the fringe far right. The world is changing too quickly to afford to go backwards right now. Canada needs a strong Conservative party to balance our democracy, however, they keep pandering to the far right fringe and picking unelectable leaders."

Sarah jumped in as soon as Sam finished, "I am fearful, Sam; look what happened in the States. Partisan politics got a populace leader elected. It could happen here as well."

Jo had raised her hand to get in the conversation, "I feel like a school girl again, ha."

Sam joked, "You look like you could still be in high school!"

"Thanks Sam. What I was going to say is, like in Alberta, there are a lot of people in western democracies who are fed up with their governments. They are angry and they don't know what to do. As a result they protest feeling no one is listening to them."

"And blame Trudeau, or whatever leader, for everything they see wrong in their lives, love. It is the same in the UK and all over Europe where neo-nazism is raising it's ugly head. Maybe even worse than here in North America. People don't feel in control of their lives anymore."

Sam had poured himself another glass of wine, filling up Sarah's glass at the same time. "My old man used to say that the best form of government was a democracy with a benevolent dictator at the top to step in to control any silly ideas of the politicians."

Sarah pointed out, "Look at all the trouble caused by autocrats though, like Jo said. Look at countries like North Korea, Myanmar or China where it isn't religious based like Iran. No, democracies may be flawed, but as long as they have checks and balances in their systems, they are still the best systems for the people."

"We all need to feel in control of our lives. It's the need for power and the pursuit of it that always ends up screwing countries up." Jo continued, "Has there ever been a truly benevolent dictator?"

Sam answered, "Probably not. And it's always the poor general public that have to suffer through these ego-maniac power crazies like Putin in Russia." Sam looked at the blue eyes of the three women and decided to check the waters by asking, "Is the problem that we don't have enough women in leadership positions and that is why there are so many problems in the world?"

There wasn't the reaction Sam hoped for, only general agreement. Bryony summed it up, "No doubt the world needs more Angela Merkls and Jacinda Aherns, but it is starting to happen more. It's difficult for women to get there, plus I don't think we are as programmed to seek power and control as men are. But good try, Sam. Thought you would get us going eh, love?"

"You got me there." Sam had a big smirk on his face. Sarah realized he was now completely comfortable with her friends, which made her feel really good. The wine he kept pouring in her glass didn't hurt either.

As the night was drawing to a close, Bryony was in the rocker feeding Aurora. Jo said, "There is still one topic we've avoided all week and you two leave tomorrow. Sarah, how are you really doing after, you know, your horrible experience. The rape?"

Sarah didn't like it when she was asked about this. She also knew she did need to talk about it and there were no better people to do it with than where she was right now. "I'm doing well, I think."

From the rocking chair Bryony called out, "On the surface, yes Sarah, you are doing great. But inside? A cynic might say you surround yourself with two lesbians and an old man who could be your grandfather. No offense, Sam. But Sarah, love, do you see what I mean?"

"B., I have thought about what you say. Sam has been better to me than my parents and you and Jo…it's the same. I love you guys." Tears were coming down her cheeks. "I don't think I am hiding behind you as protection. I know I still need to deal with this and will carry it the rest of my life. I had a moment on this last kayak leg while standing under a beautiful waterfall with Sam. My self-confidence is better now than it has ever been and the falls and swimming in the sea everyday have made my body and mind feel whole again."

Sam said, "She skinny-dips." He was always trying to get a reaction or a laugh.

Jo apologized, "Sorry for that, Sarah. We also love you and we're naturally worried about our good friend. What you say is reassuring. We'll still watch over you like mother hens, ok?" Jo had moved around the table to give Sarah a hug and dry her cheeks with the backs of her hands.

Sarah felt that her tear-ducts had just released more of the pain and anger from her assault. In Jo's embrace she felt warmth and the love she received from all three in the room. "Jo, I shuddered when you asked that question. Now I am glad you did because this experience tonight just built me stronger. And no, I don't think I'm hiding behind you three. I am still finding myself and trying to be as good a person as I can with you guys as my target models."

"What do you mean, she skinny-dips, Sam?" Bryony was burping Aurora now.

"I don't know. Sarah, is it to get the most cleansing out of the experience?"

"Sam, I think it is. I'm sorry. It just happened and I felt like it needed to continue that way. I'll bring a bathing suit with me when we continue tomorrow."

-29-

The start the next morning was later and slower than it should have been due to the previous night. Sarah's head fog told her she'd had too much wine. The good part of the night had been the last conversation that turned out to be good for her soul.

Jo suggested that with the late start they should launch from Island View Beach which would give them about a four hour paddle to Portland Island, the destination for the night. The Suburu was fully loaded with Sarah and Bryony in the back seat with Aurora. Sam got to ride shotgun beside Jo this time. Thirty minutes later they were at the launch site at Island View Beach.

Sarah felt a bit like a tourist attraction while loading all their gear and food into their kayaks. This beach is popular with walkers taking advantage of the kilometers of beachside trails. The walkers and their dogs were constantly stopping to watch them and ask questions about what they were doing.

Once ready to go it was time to say good-bye to Bryony and Jo. Buried in enthusiastic hugs Sarah and Sam thanked them for their hospitality and a lovely week of meals and conversation. Before they knew it they were on the water again, having to switch their brains to kayak mode. While it was far more sheltered here than it had been on the west coast, one still had to pay attention to tides and currents and wind forecasts. The swells of the outside were no longer a consideration. Now they had to be always aware of boat traffic and would try to avoid commercial routes altogether.

As they approached the southern point of James Island, Sarah looked back to see Bryony and Jo still standing on the beach to watch them as they disappeared between James and Sidney Islands. Sarah and Sam waved by raising their paddles receiving full arm waves in return.

Several sport fishing boats plied back and forth on the east side of James Island, so they angled northeast toward the cliffs of Sidney Island. A ten-knot wind pushed them gently along getting them to a pee break at Sidney Spit on the northern tip of the island. From there they could see Portland Island with all the ferry and boat traffic from Swartz Bay and Canoe Cove.

It was a bit of a zig-zag route to paddle to Forrest Island and then over to Coal Island before going to Portland Island, but this route provided the most shelter and avoidance of boats. Most boaters are very careful around kayakers. Every so often they would get too close so Sarah and Sam would have to turn their bows into the boat wake for a short roller coaster ride before readjusting their course back towards their destination.

Portland Island is a Provincial Park and has three camp-sites. Sarah and Sam tucked in behind Hood Islet to see if there were any spaces at the southern most campsite. "We've lucked out again, Sam. The place is all ours."

Sam chuckled, "No luck involved. It's good clean living and a will to win."

"Right." Sarah gently slid her kayak onto the midden beach in front of the campsite. Heading to the wooden toilet she noticed how nice the campsite was laid out with picnic tables and cedar rail fences marking each site. Sam met her on the trail to the camps, so they decided to pick out their site before going back to the kayaks to start bringing everything up. They chose a site with a huge arbutus tree hanging over one side, it's red trunk strikingly different from its dark green leaves and white flowers. They set up camp as a BC Ferries ship slid past them on it's way to Tsawwassen and Vancouver.

An information board showed them the over ten kilometers of trails on the island and explained some of its history. Sarah found out more on her cell phone. Walking the trails they discovered fruit trees, roses, and gardens that had been made by the Hawaiians who settled on the island around 1880. Every beach they came to was a midden made by the First Nations people over thousands of years. Stopping at the north end of the island to sit atop a cliff looking towards Saltspring Island, Sarah read from her cellphone, "Portland Island was named after Admiral Moresby's flagship, the HMS Portland. He was the Pacific commander from 1850 to '53. It was given to Princess Margaret, Elizabeth's sister, in 1958. She gave it back to BC in 1967 as long as it stayed a park. That's why no one lives on it now. It had feral sheep on it until 1980 when they were removed."

Still gazing at Saltspring Sam grunted, "Hmmph. Interesting history this island. That electronic device of yours isn't totally useless!" He was always giving Sarah a hard time about her cellphone. It would be always in reach of a tower on this side of Vancouver Island. She had hardly ever brought it out on the west coast where they relied on the three amp hand-held radio.

That night at the campfire Sam said, "In Victoria I was wondering if you were going to keep going on this trip. Paddlin' with an old man when you have so much else going on in your life."

"Never came to my mind, Sam. I couldn't abandon you now!"

"Oh, so you just feel sorry for me."

"Responsible is more like it!" Sarah and Sam both laughed, then she said, "We have to complete this for your dad. Besides I'm not leaving anything undone again in my life. And I've still got healing to do. You have to help me figure out what to do with my life, besides being a landlord now. Did you consider stopping?"

"Not for a moment. I guess I feared you'd stop to live your life in Victoria. I decided I'd continue regardless. I'm sure glad you're still with me, although we are an unlikely pair. I could be your grandparent!"

"Sam, truth be told, you are more like a parent to me than mine were. For me it's a stroke of luck I ran into you and Pete at Kaikash. I love you guys!"

"If he was with us he'd say the same about you. And I feel the same. Just don't call me Dad."

"OK, Pops!" After more laughter, Sarah got a serious look on her face and raised her cup, "To Pete!" Sam raised his cup to toast with her.

The next morning Sarah woke to the sounds of Sam getting the stove going on the picnic table. She found her bikini and towel and headed to the beach for her ritual swim. It was a good thing she had brought her black bikini for this part of the trip as a ferry was coming into sight when she emerged from the water. As usual Sam didn't take much notice of her other than to express amazement that she did this, "How was it today?"

"Invigorating as ever. You should try it!"

As usual they got an early start that morning but were delayed at the islet in front of their camp by three southern resident orcas. The whales were feeding along the bottom of Hood Islet oblivious to the ferries all around them. Sarah wondered if the people on the ferries even knew why the two kayaks were rafted together. After about thirty minutes the whales moved up the west side of Portland Island not considering that the kayakers were going the opposite direction.

The paddle that day was on smooth water over to privately owned Moresby Island. There were signs up telling them it was illegal to trespass, but Sam went to shore just past Reynold Point regardless. His bladder needed emptying so Sarah thought she might just as well join him. As they started to cross Swanson Channel a large tanker was coming towards them from the south. They paddled close to shore along Moresby Island only crossing over to South Pender Island when the tanker was even with them. It wasn't long before the wake gave them a prolonged roller coaster ride.

Sam growled, "I thought they were supposed to slow down around here to help out the endangered orcas."

"They are supposed to. That bugger sure wasn't slowing down."

"What's his rush? He'll go behind Saltspring or up by Ladysmith and anchor until he can get into Vancouver anyways. Always in a rush to make money and who gives a shit what damage is done to do it. Behind them they could hear the waves from the wake smashing into the shore of Moresby as if emphasizing his point.

The cliffs along Wallace Point were lined with high end houses. Many of them had wooden stairs built down to the beach, which otherwise would be difficult for them to reach. They followed a steady stream of boats into Bedwell Harbour, North Pender to their left and South Pender to their right. At Poets Cove they saw what all the boats were doing there. Loud music from the shore, banners welcoming everyone, with boats moving in all directions possible made Sarah and Sam stay close to the shore with the kelp beds and sea gulls as company.

At the top of the harbour was a narrow canal that separated the two Penders. The islands were connected by a bridge that the kayaks slid under into Browning harbour on the north side of the bridge. They had talked about perhaps camping on Pender for a night, but so many people around pushed them to paddle on. Sarah knew of a relatively new campsite on the top of Prevost Island that supposedly had a composting toilet. Prevost had formerly been all privately owned, but recently properties had been bought or bequeathed to or by the Province of B.C.. She knew James

Bay was a popular anchorage, but this early in the spring she hoped there wouldn't be too many campers as the boaters slept aboard their crafts.

Two hours after leaving North Pender they rounded Peile Point to enter James Bay. "Sarah, why are there two James Bays?" Sam didn't like repetition like this.

"Just lucky I guess, Sam. Wow, look at all the boats anchored in there. Want to go back and camp just below the point on the outside?"

"You read my mind. Telepathic now are we? Another skill to add to the resume. The beach looked ok when we went past. Let's go back."

That night they sat watching ferries coming and going through Active Pass, amazed that ships that large could fit into such a narrow passage. They sounded their horns as they entered to warn other boats they were about to enter the pass. Twice Sarah and Sam witnessed ferries that were going in opposite directions negotiate their way past each other. From their vantage point the ships looked only meters apart. They knew they were further apart than that, but they also knew the tidal currents were wicked through that pass as the Salish Sea flowed into the Gulf Islands or vice versa. They were left in awe of the skill of those captains, which kept them watching until dark sent them to their tents.

Sarah came out of her tent as the sun rose over the Coast Range, illuminating Mount Baker and making the old volcano look far closer than it was. She had her oversized towel wrapped around her while making her way to the water for her morning ritual swim. The high tide meant she didn't have far to go. The water felt warmer here on the inside encouraging her to swim out into deeper colder water. To increase her therapy factor she pulled her bikini top up freeing her breasts to fully experience the front crawl out into still deeper water.

Thinking she had gone far enough she turned around to swim back. Half way in she lifted her head to see a man standing there holding her towel. It wasn't Sam. Panic flooded her mind as she readjusted her bikini and continued to slowly swim in. "That's my towel." Closer now she noticed this man was tall and handsome. A threat or not?

He answered, "I know, I saw you go in. My camp is just around that little point." He was pointing down the beach. "I was going to give it to you at the edge of the sea. When you got out."

"OK." Probably not a threat then. Sarah kept swimming in keeping her eye on him.

"I don't know how you can swim in that cold water, especially in the morning when the sun is barely up."

"I only recently discovered it. It's therapy for the body and mind." As her feet hit bottom he held the towel out with his hands spread wide. Sarah moved quickly to wrap the offered towel around her. "Thanks."

Sarah noticed Sam watching from the edge of their camp. "Breakfast is ready." Sam said this dripping with protectiveness.

Turning to the newcomer Sarah said, "Guess I'd better eat then. We like to get early starts for our day's paddle."

"Where are you going today?"

"Just up to the Secretary Islands. Maybe only as far as Wallace. You?"

"I am going that way, too. Mind if I join you two? I'm Marco."

Looking at Sam to get a nod, "I'm Sarah. This is Sam. Sure you can join us. Sam always says people shouldn't kayak alone."

Conditions were as predicted by the forecasts from the night before, so Sam didn't even listen to the radio as they multi-tasked breakfast and packing. Sam couldn't resist, even though he knew he shouldn't, "So Sarah. Marco, eh? He's tall, dark, and handsome."

"Really, Sam. Give me a break. I hadn't noticed." She lied, and felt an inner flutter she hadn't experienced since high school.

"Well, you know I am always available to walk you down the aisle!"

"Sam, we just met the guy. He's probably married. And I totally expect you to walk me down the aisle. In a few years, not today, so hold your horses. And pick up the pace, here comes Marco already."

As they headed up the Athol Peninsula there was a steady flow of boats heading up the side of Saltspring Island. With Sarah and Marco paddling close together in deep conversation, Sam put the radio on and was shocked by what he heard. "Hey, you two. Come here. All those boats are going to an oil spill at the top of Saltspring."

"Holy shit!" This was Sarah's go to worst expletive. "Wonder how bad it is? We've got to go help." Her inner voice was telling her this was Mother Nature issuing another warning about interfering with the natural order of things.

The two men were in agreement and a three-hour hard paddle ensued. By the time the kayakers got to the spill a tanker had stuck it's head out from behind Saltspring where it had been waiting to go fill up in Vancouver. A yellow foam boom went all the way around it. A Coast Guard zodiac told them not to get any closer.

Sarah asked, "How can we help?"

They were directed to a large group of people working on the shore, trying to save birds that had been soiled by the escaped oil. Paddling in they became aware of the blows of orcas coming along the shore towards the spill. "The whales are going right towards the oil boom!" Sarah could feel the panic in her chest.

Sam looked pale with fear, "How can they be stopped?" He turned his kayak towards the orcas as if this could stop them. "There's four of them. Two females and two young ones."

No sooner had Sam turned when several zodiacs and research vessels appeared as if from nowhere. Apparently, this was all part of the oil spill plans as underwater sirens were directed at the whales who disappeared for over five minutes before their blows were seen on the shoreline of Galiano Island, still heading north, but they were no longer in danger of swimming through the spill.

The three kayakers had rafted together and silently watched the orca incident. Sarah admitted, "I almost felt sick to my stomach with helplessness when we saw those orcas heading toward the tanker."

Marco touched her arm, "I did as well. This whole situation is off-putting because we have no control over anything here. And the southern residents are so endangered."

"The worst feeling. And it's compounded by all your memories of bad out of control personal experiences. Is that happening for you, Sarah? Breathe!" Sam was looking directly into her eyes.

Sarah had tears welling up as she glanced sideways at Marco. A deep breathe did make her settle down a bit. Turning back to Sam, "I can't control that reaction either."

Marco's voice brought her back to the present, "Let it all out. Let it go. We won't look."

Another big breath and Sarah started paddling toward the bird rescues happening on the shore. She wondered how Marco was so empathic. Like he knew exactly what the right thing was to say.

They spent the rest of the day cleaning gulls and diving ducks. Sadly, many dead birds had to be bagged and labelled. As the afternoon wore on coffee and food was provided for them. Sam was part of the bird collection team. Sarah and Marco worked together washing birds in one of the provided tubs. They didn't get to talk to each other much, other than about what they were doing. Sarah noticed how skilled Marco was with his hands and found out he was a cardiologist at the Royal Jubilee Hospital. He explained, "Actually, I don't start at the Jubilee for ten days. I have been working with the Victoria Heart Institute. This trip might be my last chance to do something like this for a while. Didn't expect I'd be rescuing wildlife as part of my trip."

"Me neither. At least I feel better that we are doing something positive."

"The other thing I didn't expect was to meet a beautiful woman out here!"

Sarah felt her cheeks heat up as she blushed. "Just keep holding that Grebe's head up and keep your attention on the job!"

"Yes ma'am! Didn't mean to over step the mark there."

Sarah looked up at Marco, feeling some chemistry here, "You are not so bad yourself."

That shut him up as they finished cleaning the Grebe so that the Vet could inspect it with Marco still holding it. Sam was now standing beside Sarah. "That is the last bird, Sarah. We should paddle over to Wallace Island for the night."

The Vet thanked them and told them they should get going while they still had light. On the short paddle over to Wallace, Sam explained to the others that the spill was just bunker fuel caused by broken seals on the main propeller shaft. "Thankfully, that was not a full tanker spill. Can you imagine the damage that would cause?"

Sarah turned to Marco, "Sam and I have talked about this a lot. We both fear the damage a bitumen spill would cause."

He replied, "I know. And all so a few people can make huge profits for a few years at the risk of destroying this whole ecosystem."

Sarah was liking this young doctor more and more.

The shore of Wallace had a thin line of oil on the west side but the east side was clean and gave them a nice campsite facing Galiano Island. Sam built them a nice fire they all snuggled around while the sun set to their left. He went to bed first leaving Sarah and Marco talking into the early morning to find out more about each other.

-30-

With Sam making bacon and eggs, Sarah headed for her swim, noticing no movement from Marco's tent. He magically appeared holding her towel for her as she came out of the water. At breakfast Marco reconfirmed that they were comfortable with him joining them for the next leg of the trip.

"Glad to have a doctor with us, son. I'm not getting any younger," Sam joked.

"Besides, I need someone holding the towel for me each morning." Sarah winked at Marco. The spark between them was obvious to Sam who kept his approval inside, because it was none of his business who Sarah took a fancy to. Sarah knew she had only known Marco for twenty-four hours, yet he had generated feelings inside her that she'd never really had before. She wondered if he felt the same. She was aware that she was searching hard for the signs. Her inner voice chastised her by reminding her they hadn't even kissed yet.

As they rounded Chivers Point to head north past the crippled freighter they were hit with a horrible smell sitting on the calm water of Houston Passage. Luckily this was the only remnant of the oil spill from the day before. Regardless, Sam suggested they go back to paddle on the east side of the Secretary Islands. It was always more interesting paddling amongst smaller islands where paddlers got to see more wildlife, and where boats didn't go.

Three hours later they crossed over to the northern tip of Thetis Island for a lunch break. Sarah and Marco had been paddling side by side all the way in constant conversation. Sam went ahead to give them space, only interrupting to point out hazards like Dodd Narrows, where they had to time the tide or when he saw eagles, kingfishers, or seals. He caught snatches of conversation as Sarah explained her experiences with the tsunami and how she had met Pete and him. He wasn't sure how much she had learned about Marco who appeared to be a very good listener.

By mid afternoon they had reached Pirates Cove Provincial Park on De Coursy Island. The cove itself had a very shallow and narrow entrance, a perfect place for a pirate ship to hide. Boats approached the entrance by aiming at an arrow and X marked on a sloped rock shelf on the shore. They then had to stay to the left of a channel marker that took them very close to the little spit guarding the harbour. It was easy for the kayaks to simply slide into the narrow entrance by skirting the shore. It was a busier campsite than Sarah would have liked, but they decided to stay anyway, finding the most removed campsite where their three tents could fit. De Courcy actually had roads on it, but few permanent residents and no ferry to it. The attraction to De Courcy was the interesting history attached to the island.

After setting up their tents Sarah joined Sam and Marco as those two set up their stove to start making afternoon tea. Sarah sat at the end of the picnic table, pulled out her cellphone and started to research the infamous Brother XII and his cult that had started a farm here after WW I.

"You guys have to hear this." Sarah was busy scrolling through her findings. "We might have to go on a search for gold coins after tea."

Marco grinned, "What are you talking about, just because it's called Pirates Cove? There's no treasure here."

Sam chipped in, "No pirates, but all my life I've heard about the buried treasure of the De Courcy Twelve."

"Well for starters there were a lot more than twelve of them. This English guy started a utopian colony here in the late 1920's. He was a small bearded guy who often was seen in a yellow Buddhist monk robe who called himself Brother XII. He claimed he was the reincarnation of the Egyptian God Osiris and that he was part of a select group of brothers that included Confucius, Buddha and Jesus Christ. His Aquarian Foundation had over 8,000 followers worldwide."

"So he had a firm grip on reality then, eh. Here's your tea." Sam had made it the way Sarah liked it.

Still looking at her cellphone, Sarah said, "Thanks. So, the people came and gave him money that he converted into gold coins that were put into over 40 jars and hidden."

Marco stopped sipping his tea, "So that's why we're going on a treasure hunt. I get it."

"There's more scandals that developed around this colony and he had another farm on the Big Island. The scandals included black magic rituals, slave labour, sex with married couples, torture, missing money and gold coins, attempted murder, and more. His partner was a sadistic priestess called Madame Zee who carried a horsewhip to intimidate and beat her slaves, the followers."

"Wow. How did they get away with it? I mean I know it was in the 1920's and 30's but…" Sam had made his point.

"Eventually the authorities caught up to Brother XII and Zee. In 1933 it was. So the two of them burned most of the colony down, sunk their flagship sailboat, and escaped to Switzerland where he is supposed to have died in 1934. Except he was seen later that year in San Francisco. Nobody knows what happened to him, her, or the gold. Lots of people have searched all over this island, but found nothing. The main dorm and barn are still standing." Sarah looked up at the two men, "We've got some exploring to do. Let's go."

Exploring the island provided more information about the cult and gave them an unusual distraction for the afternoon. One thing they weren't expecting was how many houses there were on De Coursy and how many vehicles were parked in the community lot. After dinner Sam told Sarah and Marco about the other utopian colonies around the Island including Cape Scott, Sointula, Merville and Cedar. "It was really quite a thing at the turn of the 1900's. These Europeans coming here to find utopia and start perfect lives. Or at least better. I heard of one guy who bought acreage sight unseen in the Broughton, from an add in the paper in London. It took him six months to get there to discover most of what he'd bought was a cliff. Apparently, he stayed and he logged it and slid the logs down to the sea, boomed them, and took them to Vancouver to sell. Tough old buggers back then."

Sarah said, "Imagine the look on his face after going half way around the world to see the land he bought was a cliff!"

With Sarah and Marco snuggled together around the fire, Sam went for a beach walk until dark when he slipped into his tent unnoticed by the two smiling faces lit up by the fire.

The following morning Sarah got her swim in despite a very early start to avoid as much action in Nanaimo Harbour as they could. Their route involved going north up the east side of De Courcy and Link Islands to hide behind Mudge Island so that they could avoid the danger of the very tricky Dodd Narrows. Then they followed the western shore of Gabriola Island, until crossing near Jesse Island to avoid ferries and float planes in the top of the busy harbour. In many places they saw the fantastic natural artwork caused by the rain and sea eroding the sandstone islands causing circular patterns that looked too good to be natural. Rounding Neck Point they were confronted with the wide open bulk of the Salish Sea, some twenty-two miles across here. After three hours of paddling, it was time for a short rest even though it was only ten in the morning.

Sarah had her chart out looking for the best camp spot given the late spring weather. The decision of the group was to get as far as they could today knowing that the wild kind of camping Sam and Sarah were accustomed to wouldn't be possible on the populous east coast of the Island. Sam wanted to spend their last night on "Tree Island", which Sarah couldn't find on the charts even though she was told it was near Comox. With the longer days they could stop at campsites at Rathtrevor Beach and Bowser before getting to the Comox area. With the southerly winds pushing them they should be ending their trip after three more nights. All of the paddlers started to think more about what they would do next after the kayak trip ended. For Sarah and Sam that meant the circumnavigation started by Sam and Pete would be completed. Sarah didn't know what was going to happen with Marco, but she was enjoying getting to know him. She certainly had never felt like this about anyone before.

-31-

A gentle ten knot breeze blew the three kayaks into Baynes Sound running between the big island and Denman Island. They could see the wind line in the water ahead of them, where the breeze appeared to end in calm water. California sea-lions kept popping up around them, a species they had not seen much of on their trip. These sea-lions were smaller than the Stellars' they usually encountered. They had a darker more upright head and had a large colony at Fanny Bay. The larger Stellar sea-lion males were known to crush female California's by trying to mate with them.

Baynes Sound hosted numerous oyster and other shell-fish farms. Sarah had heard, probably from Sam, that this proliferation of life provided food for dense populations of other species including eagles and kingfishers, as well as river otters and the sea-lions. As usual, Sam was busy pointing them all out to Marco and her as they moved up the Sound. He also pointed out the Arthur Erikson designed house on Denman and the home of a famous actress, who grew up in Comox, on the tip of Ship's Point.

Sarah mentioned to Sam, "I don't see this Tree Island on the charts. And what the heck are the green and red stop lights about half way up Denman?"

"There's a cable ferry between Buckley Bay and Denman. The lights stop traffic when the ferry goes by, because the cable gets pulled closer to the surface. It won't affect us. Tree Island is what we locals always called where we're going tonight. On the charts it'll be something like Sandy Island Marine Park."

"I see it now. At the north tip of Denman."

"At low tide you can walk from Denman to Tree, I mean Sandy, Island. It's a really cool place and most people living in the Valley never go there. Yet you can see it from Comox and Courtenay."

Paddling along the side of Denman, they encountered one oyster farm after another until they got to Henry Bay, a popular local anchorage. The low tide meant Longbeak Point was connected to Sandy Island. People could easily walk over from Denman. The land seemed to tower above them as they skirted along the shore, entertained by all the geoduck and clam squirts. They all laughed when a seagull got squirted and lifted off making loud squawks of protest at the personal indignity the bivalve had caused it.

The campsite at the marine park was surprisingly empty, considering how many boats and people were present. They got the deluxe campsite under two huge firs with a view across Baynes Sound to Union Bay and the subdivisions north of it. This spot was a micro-climate that trapped the heat of the sun making it the hottest place they had been on the trip. Camp was set up quickly and Sam took them on a tour of the island. "A lot of these trails are made by the deer that walk back and forth from Denman."

Sam continued to prattle on, Sarah taking note of about half of what he was saying. Her attention was now firmly on Marco who was much more into Sam's lessons on the huge arbutus trees, the asparagus plants along the northern side of the island, or the gold-crowned sparrows nesting on the southern end of the island. For such a small island, Tree Island had three definite micro-biomes. Standing on the southern tip looking towards Hornby Island, they observed a fourth ecosystem. At low tides like this there is a huge rock-strewn shelf stretching far out towards Lambert Channel. At one point Marco counted a dozen bald eagles. As Sam took them out to investigate the tide pools Marco gave up his count as there were so many eagles eating, resting atop rocks, and flying around that he couldn't get an absolutely accurate number. Sarah teased him that his counting method was unscientific.

After dinner they took their mugs of tea and walked along the beach to the northern beach to watch the sun set over the Comox Valley. With their backs against a driftwood log they wiggled a comfortable seat into the sand and enjoyed watching the tide advance up the beach, while boats went back to Comox. Sarah cocooned herself between Marco and Sam. Seals and birds added to their enjoyment as they took in different aspects of their last night on their kayak trip. Tomorrow they'd paddle less than an hour over to Goose Spit where they'd be picked up and taken to Sam's place. Jo was coming up tomorrow afternoon to take Sarah and Marco back to Victoria.

Sarah was feeling pretty melancholy about this being the last night. "Well, here it is. The end of the trip. How are you feeling about it, Sam?"

"Sarah, I don't know what to think. My mind keeps going to what I need to get done next." Sam stared into the distance.

Marco was admiring the view of the glacier and surrounding mountains. "I know what you mean, Sam. I'm trying to force myself to be in this moment, but my brain keeps going to what is next for me."

Sam pulled a bottle of Oban scotch out of his jacket. "I saved this for this moment. It'll help us enjoy the present more." He had a huge grin on his face as he poured the Oban into their now empty mugs and proposed a toast to the end of the trip.

Sarah toasted, "To the best paddling partners ever. Pete, Sam and now Marco." They clinked their mugs together. "These past months have been transformative for everyone on the coast due to the earthquake. For me even more so. Thanks to Sam and Pete I feel like I've finally found myself. My self-esteem and confidence have never been so high."

Sam observed, "And you had a lot thrown at you. Surviving the tsunami, your parents' deaths, your surprise inheritance, the sexual assault...I mean you made all that strengthen you. Many would have been crushed by it. To Sarah" he raised his mug, and they followed suit, though another toast meant their glasses had to be refilled .

"Thanks for that, Sam. The truth is I couldn't have gotten my head where it is now without all those campfire talks with you and your dad. I definitely wouldn't be where

I am without the support of Bryony and Jo. To B. and Jo."
More toasting followed.

Marco stayed silent soaking in the atmosphere, buzzing
on the scotch, and seeing a vulnerable side of Sarah he hadn't
seen before. He realized he liked the honesty. "I can't wait
to meet your two friends, Sarah. They sound like incredible people."

"They are, Marco. You'll love them. But as Sam found
out, they can be overwhelming."

Sam smiled. "That's for sure. I'd never met such intimi-
dating women before in all my life. Sarah was lucky to fall
in with them. If you could pick anyone to be on your side,
it would be those two. Have you told Marco everything
about them?"

"What do you mean, Sam? You know I don't keep secrets."

"I mean about…well you know…how they got pregnant
and everything."

"Of course I told Marco, Sam."

Marco turned toward Sarah and Sam, "She told me they
had girl power on steroids. They used their goddess powers
to achieve whatever they wanted, including having babies."

Sam also took his gaze off the view to note that Sarah
and Marco were holding hands. "Bryony and Jo are two of
the most attractive women I've ever seen. Well, other than
Sarah." That earned him an elbow in the ribs, laughter and
another toast. "Doc, has Sarah injured her hand?"

Sarah squeezed Marco's hand, smiling as she elbowed
Sam once again.

The last morning they slept in. Sam was up first making
breakfast when Marco joined him, before Sarah ran past

them to go for her last ritual swim. She swam out almost to the anchored sailboats and motor launches, before reversing to come in. As the water became shallow she started walking in, and immediately let out a roar of pain, falling forward face first into the sea. When her head came up her only words were, "Help! Holy shit! My leg!"

Marco dropped her towel and ran down the beach like an Olympic sprinter. He had Sarah in his arms as she passed out from the pain. Sam had come to the edge of the water and could see blood gushing out of her left foot. Marco was trying to elevate her foot while he carried her to lay her on her towel. Sam had laid it out before running to get the first aid kit out of his kayak. Once Marco had laid her down he could see a large piece of green glass sticking out of the bottom of her foot. Not knowing how much damage there was, he didn't remove the glass while using most of the bandages they had to hold it in place, while at the same time stopping the bleeding. Sarah was conscious now, but in a lot of pain.

Others had heard Sarah's scream and were gathered around feeling helpless to assist. A zodiac had pulled onto the beach and Sam explained that Marco was a doctor. Marco wanted her to get to a hospital as fast as possible, so they felt the fastest way might be to take the zodiac to the Comox boat ramp. A bystander had phoned for an ambulance which would be at the ramp when they arrived in twenty minutes or so. They quickly agreed that Marco should go with the zodiac and Sam would gather their gear up and get it all to Comox somehow. He would try to meet them at the hospital.

Marco carried her to the zodiac and wrapped Sarah in her sleeping bag with her bandaged foot elevated onto the side of the zodiac. Marco sat stroking her head while holding her hand. She squeezed his hand every time the zodiac bumped up and down until she passed out again half way to Comox. Marco kept watching her foot bandages turn increasingly dark red. When they reached the boat launch the ambulance was waiting for them, but the two attendants were sitting in the cab, so Marco thanked the zodiac owner and carried Sarah to the ambulance. The back doors were now open, so he went into the back of the ambulance right past the startled paramedic. He laid her on the bed and said, "Go! She's lost a lot of blood and needs surgery soon or she'll lose the use of that foot. I'm a doctor!"

As the zodiac returned, Sam had finished taking the three tents down and packed up all the gear. He was starting to carry it all close to the water's edge, making a pile of gear before loading the kayaks. The zodiac operator introduced himself as Richard and helped him carry the gear. A young couple asked if they could carry the kayaks down for him. Richard asked what Sam's plan was and listened with eyebrows raised. Richard said, "You are not towing two kayaks back. Wait here, we'll get you a ride in so you can see your daughter in the hospital." Sam didn't have time to correct Richard or question what he was doing since he was back in his zodiac and racing out to the anchored boats.

Richard was back in two minutes. "Smitty will get you into Comox in no time. He has a truck in the lot there we can put everything into for now. I've called a cab to take you to the hospital."

"Man, you don't have to do this. You've already done so much." Sam never ceased to be amazed by how much mariners looked after each other. It took the zodiac two trips to get everything onto Smitty's Nordic Tug, Riptide. Richard tied off his zodiac on the buoy that Smitty had been using and joined them for the trip to Comox. Sam found out why he came as well when they got into the marina because they put him in the taxi straight away saying they would have the kayaks and gear in the back of a red Dodge Ram in the parking lot. Sam could pick them up anytime in the next three days. At this point Sam was feeling numb and maybe noxious about all that had happened. Not a normal morning. He knew he wasn't feeling proper at all. He felt short of breath, and his lower bowel was in knots.

At the hospital Sam was guided to his "daughter's" room by a volunteer. Sarah was out of surgery and still groggy, but managed to explain much of what the doctors did reattaching tendons and repairing her foot, Marco helping with the details. She would be immobilized for a few days. Before Sarah had finished Sam started to slump down in his chair and his head fell forward.

Pointing at Sam, Sarah said to Marco, "Look. He's fallen asleep." Her words still floated in the air as Sam slid off the chair onto the floor making a weird snoring sound.

Marco was up in a flash calling for help which arrived immediately because they were in the emergency wing. "He's had a heart attack." Sarah had to watch the tense scene unfold at the foot of her bed as first Marco and then others did chest compressions until the paddles arrived. Sarah could feel the panic in her chest when the shock caused Sam's body to briefly leave the floor.

"He's got a pulse again," an elderly nurse said like it was no big deal, that she had seen too many times to count. Two huge orderlies arrived and Sam was whisked away with Marco trailing behind trying to explain who he was.

Sarah was left all alone in her room. In shock, again, she threw up down the side of her bed. This brought a nurse in who had been in the hall outside Sarah's room. She fussed over Sarah, cleaned up, and got her comfortable again. Sarah was still shaking a bit and was sweating, so the nurse adjusted her two drips and left to find out Sam's status, saying she'd report back to Sarah as soon as she knew anything.

An hour later Sarah woke up to find Marco sitting beside her holding her hand. "Marco, is Sam going to be alright?"

"Sarah, he's going to be fine. They are really good here, but he'll have to go to the Jubilee for surgery."

The code blue announcement changed the look on Marco's face and he excused himself to head off down the hall. Marco returned ten minutes later to a panicking Sarah. "His heart stopped again. They have a US Coast Guard chopper near here that will take him for surgery at the Royal Jubilee."

"Oh Marco. I feel terrible. This is all my fault."

"No Sarah. He probably would have had this infarction sooner or later. And you didn't step on a broken bottle on purpose and almost cut your foot in half! It's the idiot who dumped the broken bottle there."

"What do we do now?"

"Sarah, we wait until the doctors say you can be discharged."

"Yikes, we need to phone Jo. Tell her not to come today. I hope we aren't too late. And what about our gear and kayaks?"

"Slow down, Sarah. One thing at a time. Where is your phone?"

"On Tree Island."

"I've got mine but I don't have their numbers. I'll see what I can do to find it."

"Wait Marco. I think I remember Bryony's"

In the end, Jo hadn't left yet. Bryony promised to go visit Sam that evening or tomorrow and get back to them. Marco slept in the chair beside Sarah who slipped in and out of consciousness the rest of that day and night.

Bryony didn't call back until noon the next day. "Sam is resting well now. They gave him an angioplasty and three stents and are monitoring him in the cardiac rehab ward. Coronary artery disease they said due to cholesterol. I had to lie that I was his daughter in order to see him. His whole family is here as well. I've put them up in your house, Sarah, love. Found the hidden key under the big rhodo."

"Thanks for that, B. I get to go home tomorrow. Can Jo still come up around noon?"

"No worries, love. She'll be there at the hospital at noon. Simple as. Sam says all your gear is in a red Ram at the marina for you to pick up. Sam also said you shouldn't worry about him. He says they have cleaned him out so he's good for at least another fifty years. He claims that now he's fixed up, he's worried about all the rest of us. Typical

Sam! He says he'll still be able to walk you down the aisle. Is there something we don't know about? What's going on up there?"

Sarah could only smile and give Marco's hand a squeeze.

-32-

After her release from the ward in Comox, Sarah had Jo take Marco and her directly to the Royal Jubilee Hospital in Victoria to see Sam. Marco found a wheelchair for her, got her foot elevated, and pushed her into the cardiac recovery ward. The nurses on the front desk greeted him like a long lost relative before directing them to Sam's bed. Jo had left to go get Bryony.

Sam was sitting up in his bed reading a Daniel Silva novel. He only noticed his visitors when Sarah moved her wheelchair into position beside him.

Rather than greeting him politely Sarah said, "Sam, what are you playing at, scaring the daylights out of us like that?"

"Oh, Sarah! Good to see you, too! Marco, is she ok?"

Marco smiled at the fact these two could slip into good-natured banter in any circumstances. "Sam, you look really good for a guy that tried to die just days ago!" Sarah got out of her chair to hug Sam while standing on one foot.

While hugging her tightly Sam muttered, "We are quite the pair, aren't we? We definitely know how to complete a kayak adventure!"

Sarah sat back down with her foot raised. "I know, right. All we wanted to do was paddle around Vancouver Island. Things just kept happening to us."

Marco was counting on his fingers, "Let's see; there was Pete battling pancreatic cancer, there was the immigrant ship-wreck, then the small issue of the biggest earthquake in history, Sarah being violated, Pete passing, the oil spill, Sarah's foot, and Sam's coronary. You two are amazing."

Sam nodded his head. "Yes sir. We had some fun, eh, Sarah? So, what's up for you in the next while?"

Sarah looked at Marco, smiled, grabbed his arm and said, "Marco starts work here this week so he's going to move in with me! Then I'm going to study wildlife rehabilitation."

Afterword

After reading The Big One many people asked me to write Sarah's Story because they wanted to know what happened to her after the Tsunami. I decided to write this sequel in a more traditional style, focussing on Sarah and telling the story from her perspective. Many of the themes in The Big One continue here with more focus on the human responses to a life-changing event showing both the positive and negative reactions.

My wife, Judy, heavily edited the original draft to view Sarah through female eyes. Her input and editing skills are much appreciated. Friesen Press editors and staff once again went beyond their mandate to help this visually challenged West Coaster get his story told.

About the Author

Sarah's Story – Surviving the Tsunami is the second novel by John Davis Carswell, a follow-up to his debut novel, The Big One. A retired high school teacher, past trawler deckhand, and an outdoor hobbyist, Mr. Carswell co-founded and ran an outdoor education program in the Comox Valley, British Columbia.

Mr. Carswell currently resides in Comox, British Columbia, with his wife of forty-four years. Together they raised four children and a variety of animals on their homestead.

John volunteers in the hospital and as a bird handler at Mountainaire Avian Rescue Society (MARS) in Merville.

Printed in Canada